Some Bore Gifts

SOME BORE

GIFTS

stories

BY

A.G. Harmon

WORD GALAXY PRESS
An imprint of Able Muse Press

Word Galaxy Press

www.wordgalaxy.com

Printed in the United States of America

Library of Congress Control Number: 2017930340

ISBN 978-1-927409-97-8 (paperback)
ISBN 978-1-927409-96-1 (digital)

Cover image: "Minimal Bore" by Alexander Pepple

Cover & book design by Alexander Pepple

Word Galaxy Press is an imprint of Able Muse Press—at
www.ablemusepress.com

Word Galaxy Press
467 Saratoga Avenue #602
San Jose, CA 95129

For my father:

Roy Franklin Harmon, Jr., MD

Acknowledgments

I am grateful to the editors of the following journals where a number of these stories originally appeared, sometimes in variant versions:

The Antioch Review: "Native Language"
                          "Perfect Silence"
                          "For Your Listening Pleasure"

The Bellingham Review: "What They Left"

Shenandoah: "Some Bore Gifts"

St. Katherine Review: "Cameo"

Triquarterly: "A Thing of Beauty"

Contents

3   Some Bore Gifts

21   Man with Wife and Child

43   What They Left

61   Native Language

81   Cameo

115   A Thing of Beauty

149   Perfect Silence

169   In Lieu of Flowers

195   For Your Listening Pleasure

Some Bore Gifts

Some Bore Gifts

J UAN JULIO COULD DESCRIBE THE MISFORTUNE with a soft
clarity, so that the impression he left upon the listener was
that of a tune hummed from a porch step, during the long
liquid hours of the first, floating dark.

That it was a brutal and tragic tale did not diminish the
gentleness of its comprehension, such was Juan Julio's skill. Neither
did the fact that it was a steaming, hundred-degree day, heavy as
the rain clouds that ballooned about the sky above the pasture.
As his men labored at a distance, sawing and trimming out tree
foliage that threatened the power lines, he told the story again,
and the old man at his side—a doctor to whose farm the crew had
been sent—stood privy to the pressure of Juan Julio's romance.

"They sent us after the hurricane, down to a place too far from
the city for the cameras to come, too far from the sea for people to
know of. Old people lived there—the old, poor ones—the kind
who cannot be driven from their homes, even by the promise of
more to eat and less to do and a cooler place to do it in. The old
poor ones who will not surrender what they have always seen,
even if it is the worst of things. They live very close to the world
they know, these people, and must be left alone there—even by
those who come to offer more. No good can come of that, even
if good is meant."

The drone of the saws lamenting against the green wood drew closer, made it harder for Dr. Priest to hear. So the old man stepped within a few feet of the Mexican, and positioned himself so that his best ear was nearest the tale.

Dr. Priest had lived his whole life in this town, the last half of it on this farm, and had never met a Mexican. But these five were all from down there, as was every other man who came to the place now—to haul horses, to fix water mains, to read the meter. They worked from a white service truck, with a cherry picker to lift one man up to the level of the interlaced elms, hackberries, and sumacs that crowded the phone lines. As this man toiled from the bucket with his saw, two others labored on the ground, to clear the falling debris and feed it into a wood chipper. Down on the road that faced the doctor's land, a fifth drove a tractor with a boom cutter. A platform of blades whirled at the end of an arm reaching from the machine to the bordering trees. Even at a distance, the savage munch and chop of the low-lying limbs made Dr. Priest wince—made his small, rheumy eyes tear.

"So they sent us after the hurricane," Juan Julio continued, "streaming down the branch-filled roads in our trucks, caught in the trail of the storm's pull—to this land that was more cage than world, trapped within its own being—as though the whole place had sat upon a cloth, and that cloth upon a table. And then, at some moment, the four corners had been taken up, to let all that lay upon the surface plunge in upon itself, this way and that—over and under and against—until it made no sense anymore. They sent us there with orders to make the world straight—to make even that for which we had no north or south, and of which we knew no history—none with which to make what was into what had been."

Juan Julio wiped his forehead with the meat of his forearm, so that the flesh glistened in the early afternoon light.

He was as tall as Dr. Priest had been, before age had stooped him. But besides his status and his formal air, there was a marked difference between the foreman and the others. They were little and mustachioed, and they veiled their black eyes beneath dusty, close-fitting caps. But he was clean-shaven and hatless, his hair cut short in a military style. He wore crisp khakis and a fresh polo shirt. Only his boots showed the scuff that might be expected. His eyes were bright and direct, and though he had an accent, his English was smooth, schooled; Dr. Priest could not understand the others.

"What you see now," Juan Julio pointed to the workers, "we did then, there, in that place. Except the earth was no longer set out in the squares that mark men's claims."

The chain saw broke through the circumference of a limb, so that a mighty crack sounded as the blade caught its breath. The two men on the ground struggled to untangle the fallen bough from the lower foliage. Then a gloss of new sunlight broke onto the pasture, free to bathe the weeds and fescue.

"It would have been all right," Juan Julio said, "had we been the same kind of people. In a strange place, there must be something you can count on. The men beside you must know the things you do."

"These you see here," he said, and pointed to the workers, "these with me, they all come from my village in Nuevo León. They have done this work a long time, and each knows his role. With a duty such as ours, with a task such as that, to make the world even and plain, there is no room for questions. The problem is what to do, not how to do it, where to start—not how one starts."

Juan Julio frowned, considered what he had said. Then he remade his point.

"As my grandfather told me, in a battle, the questions are small: from which direction to fight—head-on or from the flank?—but not how to hold a sword. The men must already know such things; they must be soldiers by that time, not still farmers."

He stopped, wiped his brow again. Dr. Priest stepped closer.

"But we were not the same men."

Because those they sent were of all types, all skills, and many were not fit for the task. They were men for different times, for a known world—men who worked with hand tools, who sawed lumber from a mill, who masoned brick fresh from a mold, or managed water that ran within pipes. The work they did only made sense when the place itself did, when houses lined streets, and trees rose from mown grass. They were not men for a place with no line between outside or in—when water lapped at windows, and trees lay down like the slain. Even the men from Juan Julio's crew were unsure of their way, though clearing the land was their native task.

"Even *we* had to scrape the earth," said Juan Julio, "to find traces of a drive, a road, a curb—some paved corner that would tell us where to lay the teeth of the saw."

It was as though they were chipping away at an ice wall, to uncover the bones of a primitive beast, or sweeping the floor of a pit, to reveal the stones of an ancient culture—trying to retrieve a thing or a place that the earth had swallowed up with its slow brown mouth. In such times, when even the master is unsure of his craft, it is madness to employ the novice—and criminal to arm him with means.

"But that is what happened," said Juan Julio.

In fact, they all suspected the days themselves lay under a spell, as if the confusion of the landscape had broken in upon the fabric of a recollected life, breached the judgment of those who—at any other moment in the regular course of existence—would know better than to mix such unlike things, or to permit so careless an enterprise. Their wits, dazzled by what they saw, made fools of the lot, so that if a mere child had presented himself at the dawn of a day's labor, he would not only have gone unchallenged, but would have been fitted straight away with a blade broader than his waist, and manned with a canister of gas, a box of matches.

"We were dizzy with fatigue, and our thirst could not be slaked, though we drank constantly. The work we did was poor, careless, including that of the skilled. The best of us gave place to the least, and even a good job begun would likely end in frustration—broken tools, lack of oil, lost directions."

Juan Julio swallowed.

"But mostly we were frightened, milling about in the footprints of a monster, clearing the ruin of her wrath. And no matter what they told us, who could say that she would not turn back, retrace her steps, come for those who erased the marks she'd meant to leave? We slept in fits, fought often. Hate came easily."

More than once Juan Julio had studied a man's neck, then gauged the size and strength of his own hands.

"I am ashamed of this now," he said, looking away. "But it is true, and I tell it to atone for what I desired."

Dr. Priest closed his eyes, nodded. He had been in war. He had known the same thing that the Mexican spoke of, and had done worse than just ponder it. Not only had he done worse, what's more, he had lived to know of other things, worse yet.

"It was a hazy day," said Juan Julio, his voice rising to the pitch of the saws.

"None of us mentioned the pale fog that hung in the air, but we noticed and worried why it should be. Was it fire, eating its way toward us, silently—a blaze that would all at once send flames from the tangled brush, at a point too late to run?"

But they could not smell smoke. So was it rain? The mist of some early child of a storm, thrust from the giant's hollow, now growing into a menace of its own—to undo what little good they had realized?

"But the clouds were high that day, and the wind was docile. So how could it be rain?"

Still, there it hung, as though they had stepped within a curse for which they were ignorant of both the deserving and the unfolding. All day they rubbed their eyes, waved their hands before their faces—but none spoke of what he saw.

Perhaps that was why they misunderstood. They had thought that the meaning of the day would be related to the purpose of the haze; that what fogged their sight would prove their undoing; if not of all, then of some; if not of some, then of only one. Perhaps it was this error that had caused what happened, because they were so intent upon the source—fire, water, evil—that their attentions were divided; the mélange of half-skills and muddled wits, the lack of a voice to speak to, or to bring order from, the chaos that surrounded them. Engrossed, absorbed, they had looked for the mist to mean something, and had been caught unawares, facing the wrong way.

Juan Julio turned to the road, pointed to the tractor that inched slowly along the border. The arm at its side held out the flat mouth of blades, like a head at the end of a neck—like the unhinged jaws of a reptile to the trapped and waiting trunks. Dr. Priest's gaze followed the man's finger; the tops of the trees quaked as the violence tore at them from beneath.

"I had been working with the tractor, guiding the boom so that it lay against a snarl of trees and undergrowth. The arm would catch at times, buck and bounce, when placed against a mass too thick for it to eat. Two men trailed behind me, pulling away the cuttings and piling them into heaps. I could not see them, but I knew that they were there."

The work was slow, the man explained; twenty feet an hour, along a roadside they had discovered the day before.

"The people to whom the road led had been trapped, cut off from supplies, and it was feared they would stay there, starve and rot, rather than leave their shacks unattended. So we worked on, all day. There was no rest. Without a word to each other, we began to take odd turns at the labor—the shifts unequal in both length and difficulty."

From time to time, some man or woman, filthy and wide-eyed, would step out from the wooded maze with a can of some sort—for gas or water—and tell of the need that lay behind them, in the direction in which they were headed.

"I am not sure if that was on that day; but it seemed as though I worked so long that the shudder and rattle of the machine leached through my skin and into my bones, so that it shot through and burned them—as though I held fast to an electric wire; as though the wire held me."

He stopped, smiled. His eyes broke free of their frozen width.

"That is what they say it is like, Doctor. Is it not?"

The old man nodded; so he had heard; like your skin, meat, vessels, your very heart, were being sifted through a wire screen, pulped and pulsed through a grill. Once, as an intern, he alone had been made to sit with a room full of electrocuted men. The metal scaffold upon which they were working had been pushed into a transformer. There was nothing that could be done but watch them convulse, writhing as the mortal shock tossed them about from within, like an animal trying to free itself from a cocoon.

"At some point, I stopped, climbed down; I do not remember whether I meant for someone to relieve me. I do not recall asking for such a thing. But I remember stepping aside as someone brushed past, climbed into the cab, started the motor, then the cutter."

He continued to point toward the road; Dr. Priest watched on—as the tractor crawled, as the cutter gnawed.

"Why did I do that?" he asked the old man. "Step away? I cannot answer. I remember walking off, my back to the business behind, as if my home lay on the other side of the trees, and my wife had called me to supper. I remember that I stopped, surprised to see my feet, and wondered how I had come to be there. I put my hand to my head."

He did so again, brushing his brow as if the doctor had asked him to repeat the gesture, so as to unfold the symptoms of some malady.

"They tell me that I had worked for eight hours, straight. They tell me that I had taken no water. Those things I cannot remember, though I recollect the size of my tongue. What is true, it is impossible to say now. Because though I did not see it, as I stood there, the new man in the cab lurched the machine forward, so that it bucked on its axle, one wheel catching and spinning in the mud."

The Mexican turned sideways, threw out his hip to mimic the thing's massive pitch.

"The boom snapped the pins that held it fast, so that it swung free, turned back on the two men behind. One leapt clear; but not the other."

The thing destroyed the man in a scale of ways, as though it could not decide on the right manner in which to kill him. His arm, shorn from the shoulder cap, was slung into the cleared space, where it laid there, stretched out properly, formally, while the flesh of his back and side were chewed, as though by a pack of savage dogs. Then there were two great slashes, one from the man's ear to his chest, stopping at a point halfway; the other from his collar to his hip, almost clean through, so that he lay on the ground in a curve, like a spring coiled at an angle upon the grass.

"It was a neat death, the cuts so great that the blood came in gouts rather than showers. He died with his remaining arm curled beneath him, his face held in his hand, and that hand upon the earth. As if he were ashamed of the way he had ended. As if his wounds were his sins, and he must hide his eyes from judgment."

When Juan Julio was finished, he stepped back from the old man. The tale itself might have laid upon the ground, marked with stones—a small cairn of sorrow.

Dr. Priest observed the silence, or such of it as there was. The men were still laboring in the trees. But even after a few moments had passed, and the workers were further down the way, he could not bring himself to ask more. Juan Julio had finished, and to call him back to the story would be an offense. Dr. Priest had always respected the delicate, spun sugar quality of endings.

Still, as the sun lumbered through the sky, and as he made his way back through the shadowless pasture to the house—the crew having finished for the day—the old man wondered about the one who had died.

What had they done with his body, way out there in the heat, so far down in the bayou? Even here, hours north of the Coast, they had lost power for a week and had been stranded for days on end. Isolated, what had they done with the remains?

He opened the door to the house, stood in the kitchen to let the frigid air dry his sweat into a carapace. He didn't feel like ending the day just yet. With a glass of iced tea, he went back outside and sat on the gallery swing.

It was the time of summer when the light barely surrendered the sky; hours from now, there would still be hours yet before full dark. Night was a scarce thing, but he scarcely missed it.

He would never have believed that possible. Once, it was all he had longed for: a cloaked, unbroken chain of rest, with no calls to rouse and summons, had been such a rare thing. Now, his wife had to badger him from his chair in the late evenings, force him to sleep in the bed. He rose well before dawn; he kept the house lit.

From his vantage in the swing, he could view one of his favorite sights—his small herd of Angus making its way back from a pond in the far pasture. Once raised for profit, now they were a hobby—in truth, even less; now they were part of a vignette, something to adorn the property. The noise for the past few days had disturbed their routine, driving them across the field to escape it. But with the men gone, they seemed to have settled down again. The line moved lazily back to the upper grasses, to resume their constant, singular task.

He set the swing into a gentle rock, pushing off with his toe.

At some point in the coming days, Dr. Priest would find a time to ask Juan Julio his questions. What was the man like? for example; the one who had died. Did Juan Julio know him? Was he even a man? For the Mexican called all of his workers "men," when two of them were clearly no more than boys. And most importantly, what had become of the driver? Was he punished? Sued? Did he go mad with grief and guilt?

The sun was reaching the point in the afternoon when it fell level with the roofline, and hence shot a cannon of light beneath the gallery eaves. For the time being, it only blazed across his feet and shins. But soon the glare would drive him from his place.

He lifted the glass and ran it along his forehead, then down the sides of his cheeks. He had begun to sweat again, despite the ceiling fans that hung down from the gallery roof.

There would be a moment he could ask such things, about the man, about Juan Julio; there was still much work to do. The pasture was long, and the other side of the property was ribboned with another set of lines that had to be cut back as well. Juan Julio and his crew would return.

They had taken a liking to each other from the first, he and the Mexican; at least Dr. Priest had fancied as much. He would admit this was partly due to the fact that he enjoyed any new thing that presented itself in a day. It had been such a long time since he'd had a reason for his rising.

But on the first day, they had come unexpectedly. His wife had sent him to see who was at the door. Juan Julio stood outside the foyer, formally, as though he'd come for a visit. He'd explained that the town had hired and sent them; that it was time to care for the lines. Five years had passed, by the municipal schedule, since the trees had been cut back. They had to be shorn.

Dr. Priest, then and there, had said that his wife did not care for such things. She valued her trees, no matter how far across the farm they traveled, no matter whose power was threatened by their height. He'd related how others had butchered the foliage before, turning branches into stubs and knobs, leaving the whole avenue of trees ragged and unsightly. The Mexican listened, respected such a thing, even agreed with it. Then he invited Dr. Priest to watch them, to object if their work was severe.

The schedule of the men's work saved him from the confusion his days had become since his practice was closed; a confusion that was worse now, not better, as all had said it would be. Worse with every year, in fact, and it had been many since he quit. It seemed that a door was always closing these days—things of any purpose being wrapped up and handed along. He could not content himself with avocations—sports, books, horses, even his cattle—and pretend that they were a life. This annoyed him greatly. He would not admit it, but he longed for things to break—pipes to freeze in the winter, roof tin to blow from the barn—so that he could call for repairmen to come, and then follow the workers as they plied their crafts. So when Juan Julio arrived with his crew, unbidden, it was a great and welcome surprise.

Every morning, the old man showered, had his coffee, dressed for the heat of the coming day. To discourage mosquitoes, he pulled his athletic socks to his knees, where they met the hem of his baggy shorts, so that he looked like a small, knickered boy. He wore T-shirts given to him by grandchildren, ones that needed shrinking to fit—team logos emblazoned on the front—a baseball cap and dark glasses. Then he went out to meet them, down to the end of the road, with keys to open the gate. There was a mist in the air, thick as bees, as though the sun had walked the earth before his rising, left traces of itself in the light, like pollen floating in dew.

What he had said that afternoon, Juan Julio—of the storm, of the man split in two—was only the latest tale he'd related. Over the days that had passed, the Mexican spoke of other catastrophes: a dustbowl at the border, with men hanging on the axles to cross; a gang of bandits, skulking like trolls beneath a bridge, to take a cut of their earnings when they passed. But more often, Juan Julio spoke of his endeavors, his skill at commerce. The poles about the fence rows were draped with three lines, and as the men cleared them with patience and care, Dr. Priest heard of the younger man's endeavors.

"I bought my first truck with five year's earnings," Juan Julio had said. "My second, I bought with the earnings of three. I brought up more men from my village, along with my brother, who watches the second crew, just as I do these."

It turned out that he nearly had money for a third, what with the extra funds the government had paid him for working after the storm. He spoke of all these things with a charming pride.

Whenever they broke for lunch, the men sat at the fence line, wrapped in the shade they were soon to destroy, and opened iceboxes. Dr. Priest would leave them, return to the house for a time. There, as he picked at the meal his wife had cooked too much of, he would explain the progress being made. But whenever he heard the still heat broken by the saw's wail, he'd reseat his cap upon his plastered hair and set out for the pasture again. Sometimes he brought them lemonade or iced tea; sometimes he brought them the rest of a cake his wife had made.

"If my men get drunk," Juan Julio had told him, "they stay home. They make their choice. They don't eat if they don't work. If they chose to drink instead of eat—all right—they do as they wish. But they don't work, beg though they do. They are responsible for themselves. They owe me nothing, but then I pay them nothing."

The men were careful around Juan Julio, and he watched them like a schoolteacher. He said he collected them for mass on Sundays, and took them to the hospital if they absolutely had to go. But he himself kept a case full of medicines and antiseptics for their minor illnesses. This he had Dr. Priest review, to see if his store was adequate for the purpose.

It seemed that Juan Julio would speak to his men only when it was time to move the truck, or when it was time to take a break. Dr. Priest had even asked the Mexican why they needed such a scarcity of instruction. It was because he had trained them so well. And he knew so well how to train them because this was how he had started.

"For years I cut, I cleared, I drove the machine. But with a difference," he had said, between him and the others. "I saw more than my hands."

The cattle were all back in the field now, bloated with water, heads declined for the grass. He heard his wife stirring in the house, a business that never ended; he was envious, and sometimes aggravated, that her life had never transformed, never changed. He got in her way, now that he had no way of his own, but her path was the same as it had ever been.

He leaned out from his seat to see the browned foliage of a dead evergreen at the corner of the house. That afternoon, before the men had left, he had asked Juan Julio to cut it down. It had been a Christmas tree thirty years ago. There was a picture of it in a drawer or book somewhere, decorated with lights and balls, and a message along the white border: "tree at corner of house." A live spruce of some sort, it was a better choice for Christmas than it was for the yard, as it had grown twice as tall as the roof, and its jealous breadth crowded the way around. But a drought the summer before had killed it, and now it shed heaps of brown needles and the wind snapped its desiccated branches. Dr. Priest offered Juan Julio fifty dollars on the side if he would remove it.

He leaned back in the swing, drank the last of his tea.

Tomorrow, he would take the tree down, for two twenties and a ten—a week's wages, when he was in his training. But a man like that could make a great deal from so little. A man like that knew how to get along.

He rattled the ice against the glass.

It used to be that way for Priest himself. He cleared; he cut; he cleaned.

Now, when stillness is all that is asked of him, he recollects nothing but motion, as though in all the years before he had been hooked to a line, one that had rushed him through a torrent of borderless, numberless days. Then, he had been all hands, all eyes, all feet. Now, he moved through their recollections like a man through a museum. They limn out from shadow, and his fingers itch at their sight.

There was the child he had seen on a table, as though sleeping, except that the flesh of his trunk was peeled back, his organs, shy and small, still as a stopped clock. And a rodeo rider, calm as pond water, sitting on a gurney, though a bull had hooked a horn into his mouth and out through the orbit of his right eye. There was Dr. Priest's son, a child, curled and sleeping in the wheel wells as Priest drove through the night to make calls—in the days when you went to houses, in the days when they came to yours. With his wife sleeping next to him, he had handed syringes through the window to a man needing tetanus shots; he had stepped on a nail in a junkyard, and had knocked on the window to rouse him. There were people full of water, so bloated he'd been forced to use a bucket to bail it all out; there were children fed through a feed mill augur; a girl, ravaged by a hog; a man's face, split open by an oak plank shot backward from a planning table—his frantic eyes staring out on either side of a cracked skull, demolished nose, cleft palate—Priest had run a wire through his cheeks to stabilize his face. Stab wounds on Saturday nights, lungs near collapse, tubes pushed through to inflate them. The poor had born gifts—turnips, collards, pole beans; they had known his father, they had known his grandfather; he took the sacks and gave them to the orderlies, then marked the bills paid. And phone calls he would make, after tests had been run—good news to bring—that it was nothing; that it was all right; that there was time after all, years and years of a life left.

He stared at his tea glass, trying to remember why he had become confused.

Soon it will be time for supper, a thought that made him sigh. He will tell his wife he is not hungry. Then they will argue over this fact, as they do every night. In the end, he will have a bowl of cereal before he goes to bed. His appetite is that of a child now.

He will walk down to close the gate, then return to sit here, to watch for the lightening bugs. She will read by the television, talk on the phone, plans visits from their children, grandchildren. Holidays seem increasingly desperate now—too many people eager to be too nice, to stare too long. They watch him closely, gauge how much he eats, try too hard to amuse him, and wonder at his rest—is it enough, is it too much? He knows what they think; he has thought such things himself, from bedsides.

The line of the sun was nearly level with his face. He took a detached interest in its progress, as its heat climbed up his legs, his hips, his chest, like anesthesia as the table is tipped.

"You won't remember this," he would say to the man who lay there. "I'll call your name when it's over."

He shut his eyes.

The story of the hurricane had troubled Juan Julio. He sees that now. The man had wanted to tell it, and had probably told it often, if others would listen. And it was not so much that he wanted to be comforted as to understand why he had been confused, why he had climbed down and let some other take his place.

At that moment, the man had lost his peace, like a coin

dropped from his pocket, and now he wanted to make it good. He wanted that there be chances, possibilities, likelihoods that would crowd it out or give it purpose, prospects and options; he wanted assurance that there would be field upon field to work through; and even if he had not done this, he could yet do that—even if not all was accomplished today, then there was the day to come. Most of all, if he had failed, there would yet be successes.

Now he is caught in the storm, though, Juan Julio, and now he cannot see his way clear. It worries him—which is why his clothes are so clean, his hair brushed so well. Yes, he was always earnest, but he is more so now; he is meticulous to a fault, now. The Mexican will let nothing spill, will leave not a scrap of trash. His men must follow every rule, and his rigor with time is that of a saint. He is prepared, alert, and in his mind he is forever telling himself where he is, what he is doing, what he is yet to do—so that he will not be caught out again, so that he will not be found dreaming.

But he had time to atone. The more and longer he lived, the more he could tell the tale, again and again, until his labors drove it from his mind. That was what Dr. Priest wanted to say; that peace he could bring the man: that he had time. There were years yet, barring some other fate—ones in which he could work. Years for someone to expect him, and for his sheer toil to make over, reclaim, build back. He could set this bone for a bone that could not be set, cut out this mass for the one too large to cut, apply this pressure (heel of hand on back of hand, and heel of hand on wound) for that which could not be dammed. Raise the near dead, for the dead that could not be raised.

For he has seen its face, what every man fears. He has been the one to whom they held when they realized, at last, that love alone could not save them. Not their wives or husbands or children, but him—only him—when blood and history and friendship held no power against a rampant disease, a failing heart, time. And he would rise at such a thing, his muscles stiff and tight; he would rise at what they believed of him, and talk to them like an angel with a sword in his mouth.

Now, the days are full of skies that will not rain, that beg a purpose that they are not given. And he will not be let to answer, not be let to offer or speak, test or try. Like a horse in a barn that sees a field through the cracks in his door, he stamps at his place. Though he has legs still, and a heart, and lungs and blood, he will not be let to run over it, not even to stumble and fall.

Now he rises at night, ready, prepared, if only they will let him; he looks for a task, for a thing to make right, for succor to bring. If they would let him. He hunts the corners of the house, the places of recess, as if they hold a discovery, a mute cry, fraught eyes. He could be ready; he would need little. He had restored a man's wind with a penknife; he had tied off a vein with bailing twine.

They must be let through, he had decided. The lines must be let through—to carry answers, voices, questions put. Though they damaged and distorted the living—broke between the green, pulsing world with their naked purpose—their way must be cleared. They ran between things, and they must be prepared, stand and wait for their time. They must be ready, as he was, always, even now, to say to those who called, who held up the bright, red water of their need: be still; bring me the light; hold it here; this is the way.

Man with Wife and Child

DURING THE FOUR DAYS BEFORE he drowned while attempting to save the child, Lawrence expanded upon the discovery of his life's fulfillment.

It had been made within the span of a flight between America and the island where he would swim out to his last act. The thirty-nine years prior to those four days were completely redressed, a thought that occurred to him more than once during that period of commandeered vitality, of stolen and misappropriated completeness.

In four days, he had painted an existence beautiful enough to believe in, fraud though it might appear to be. But how it appeared to be was precisely the point.

★ ★ ★

WHEN HE WAS TWENTY-FOUR YEARS OLD, the truth had stopped sustaining him as the ground upon which he walked and the bread upon which he supped. It did not happen all at once; rather, it fell away in a continuous lapse and degradation, facts giving way to fancy, failing in consequence until nothing was left but falsehood and damnable deceit, a mirage of air-blown genie smoke.

And the thing was, he knew what he was doing. Lawrence never believed a word that he said about himself—not since he was twenty-four.

No one could have foretold his life who had seen it from its beginnings. He had started with fair promise. Of proportionate stature, he had respectable looks and was sufficient at games. He had come from modest yet comfortable circumstances, the only child of only children. He was intelligent, even gifted in areas, and his aptitude for social matters put him in good stead; conversation came easy; he was neither shy nor obnoxious.

But when he was fourteen, during the impressionable time in which his body's chemistry was in its upheaval and his mind's shell at its most permeable, a certain thing befell him. What his parents considered a prodigious imagination born from reading science fiction novels had seized upon a suggested impression. It had happened by way of an introductory class on philosophy—a "learning module," the school had called it.

Simply put, he'd been told that no one can ever know that what he's experiencing is the same thing as what others are experiencing—or for that matter, whether experience for each person is not a unique and proprietary matter—an exclusive set of pictures, sounds, and sensations as private and unknowable to others as the inside of one's own eyes.

"No one," said the teacher, an impressively thin young man in a Ramones T-shirt, "can be sure that *what* he is," he paused, "is the same as what *others* are."

Certainly there was inductive evidence, the man continued; surely we *seem* to share definitions and reactions.

"But the common identification of a stimulus is not the common experience of its effect. We may all *say* we have pain when we cut ourselves, but how do we *know* what pain *means* to another? How do we *really* know? Because he says it *hurts?* It *stings?* That only begs further questions. How do we know what 'hurt' means to him? Or 'sting'? Or any other word?"

The man smiled in a satisfied feline way.

"We *seem* to share a universe that acts upon us, but in what way that action takes its effect, we are all inextricably, and eternally, alone."

His students laughed and pretended to shiver at the proposition. But while the others dismissed the talk as soon as the class ended, Lawrence had been struck to his atoms. He had stumbled home, swallowing, trying to shake off the news as though it were the aftereffects of a high fall, the repercussions of a blow to the head. He hid his disconcertedness from his family, smuggling it into the house like a lodger hiding a gunshot wound beneath his coat.

For weeks he tried to heal the affliction, but any sense of unity he'd shared with others for his first fourteen years was lost. Tethers were sundered; he was a third species: neither human nor animal, flora nor fauna—alien—not in an otherworldly sense, but as an undiscovered, and undiscoverable, part of this world. There was no species for him, no phylum, no kingdom, here or to come.

Worse, that others did not seem troubled by the news only confirmed that *they* were all alike—that *they* were of the same state; the professor, in a sinister feat of legerdemain, had spoken what was true only of Lawrence. The evidence lay in the very fact that others went about their business, while he was troubled beyond measure or belief—to the point of conviction; to the point that from then on, it was all that he believed of himself.

Over the years, the curse would come and go, but when it came, it did so with the certainty of a secret disclosed, a fortune revealed by a sibyl too indifferent and unyielding for doubt. So he remained locked in the prison of whatever he was. Out of an overdeveloped sense of propriety and an amplified sense of fear, he felt a commensurate duty, a whispered burden, to keep the truth to himself. If he was the equivalent of the last coelacanth, he must hide the fact.

This created complications. A diffidence. He began to withdraw.

★ ★ ★

Each day after work he ate the same thing, not because he wanted it, but because he could not bear making things worse by making them elaborate. Salads, sandwiches, soup—anything prepackaged and fully cooked. He partook of it all in the kitchen, standing up, over the sink. He had a table, but it was covered with books and bags and a fan; all the chairs had coats around their backs—a makeshift closet. The only place he ever sat was in a chair, next to a sofa, in front of a television.

On the weekends, he visited a bookstore, went to the gym, shopped for groceries. Occasionally he painted on a canvas he'd been nursing for years, to pretend that it was still worthwhile. He took long naps, watched long movies.

If he was preparing to leave for the day and heard a door open down the hall, he would wait inside his apartment until footsteps rose like rain, then fell like sand, moving past his threshold.

Sometimes, he would place his eye against the peephole, to watch as the figure loomed into the concave glass, like a fish inside a bowl, then swam furiously away.

On the rare occasions when his door was already open, catching him too far outside to escape detection, he would slowly step back into his apartment rather than make eye contact with the approaching body. To defeat the strange neighbor's impression that he was just a lonely middle-aged man living inside a desolate flat on the suburbs of the city, he would pretend to be talking to someone living with him, someone far inside the apartment, who was seeing him off on his day.

"What did you want at the store?" he would call to the no one there, for the benefit of the passerby, whose face he never saw.

At work, he took to mentioning friends in conversations, though the people he mentioned were actually friends from twenty years back, and the occasions he recollected were either just as old or invented altogether. He used "we" a great deal in reference to stories he related, so that others would think he had been with someone; he rushed the telling so that no one would ask who he was with.

He had many family obligations, he said, which took him out of town a great deal. In truth, he never left town.

Many people thought that he had a peculiar, though full, routine; he was an exotic, to be sure, an eccentric but familiar type. He was cautious about living near anyone that he knew from work, because he didn't want them checking up. How much they suspected, he could not let himself consider.

He also took care of his health, because if he needed help, he would be exposed. There would be no one to come.

Above all, he knew his efforts were ultimately doomed. At some point, they would find him out. It would be nice if he were to die in his sleep.

★ ★ ★

T HE REASON LAWRENCE TOOK THE TRIP to the island was to use some of the vacation he was required to exhaust. Having no one to go with, he had a stockpile of accrued days, so many that he could have traveled around the world.

He'd picked this particular island because it was the cheapest and the least visited, and because it was possible to fly there in half a day. The villa he'd taken was secluded, so the two weeks would be pleasant enough—reading, touring, eating—though of course, alone. Still, for the time he was there, he would not have to bother with deceit.

It had happened ninety minutes into the flight, when the cabin had settled down, when drinks and peanuts had been consumed, trash gathered, conversation dulled. The passengers had either heightened their senses or deadened them, their eyes flashing at open screens or closing with pulled shades.

Ensconced in the aisle seat, Lawrence had begun flipping through the in-flight magazine, thumbing its pages for a puzzle, when the head of a sleeping child beside him fell upon his right arm.

Her small cheek was as warm as a plate left in the sun.

Surprised, Lawrence searched the girl's exhausted face—mouth wide, slack, drool pooling at her bottom lip.

Her mother was asleep against the window, a youngish woman with a fraught look, even in slumber. She wore a yellow sundress and sandals. In her lap was a cloth bag she clutched in both hands, as though it, above all things, must be kept safe.

The girl herself had thick black hair, cut in the shape of a cap. She wore little overalls and tennis shoes like any other child, but there was an elegance to her size, and to the luminescence of her skin. She seemed a thing of blown glass, something to be tiptoed about. So Lawrence remained quite still to keep her from shattering.

But what changed the rest of his life—his remaining four days—was what happened next. For when he glanced up from his study of the girl, he found himself being watched by an old woman across the aisle, a row ahead.

She smiled broadly, looking over the rims of her glasses in delight.

She's adorable, mouthed the woman.

Lawrence blinked, stared, then blinked again several times, as though he'd found himself taken in a sudden rainfall.

Adorable, mouthed the woman, her eyes squeezed tight.

An unfamiliar smile spread across Lawrence's lips; he found himself nodding.

How old?

He looked down. Four? Five?

The fingers of his left hand spread; he held them up.

The woman winked.

So precious, she said, turning away.

But in the act of leaving him to his privacy, she said one thing more, with her eyes.

Lucky. You're a lucky, lucky man.

The child slept on; Lawrence felt the soft push and pull of her rest through the fabric of his shirt.

He did not want to disturb her, to have her wake, shocked and scared by the intimacy she'd forced upon a strange man. So he would not move his head, would not scratch an itch, though of course the flesh prickled mightily beneath his nose—ants crawling down to his lip in a crooked line, then up to his nostril.

He hoped the old woman would turn around again, so he stared at the back of her head to make her feel the weight of his watch, to sense it and turn to admire him once more—him, Lawrence, and his child. But the woman had fallen asleep herself, so he had to hope for the attention of someone else.

At length, it came in the form of a stewardess, inspecting the aisles for needs. She stopped as she passed, glancing down at the small head lolling against Lawrence's arm. His heart yanked about as she noticed.

"Would she like a blanket?" The stewardess whispered.

Lawrence blushed at the yammering blood in his ears, at the swell and pound of the vein in his temple. He struggled to express a nervous thank you.

"No," he answered softly. "She's—all right. Like this."

The woman smiled.

"What about your wife?"

And it was as though a gift, perfect in every way, had revealed something unknown about itself, some aspect that made its delight all the more intense, extravagant: a box of the most lustrous mahogany opened to reveal a jewel of the most brilliant sheen.

His child. His wife.

He shook his head at the stewardess, basked in her respect. *Lucky. You're a lucky, lucky man.*

Nothing he would feel in the tropical clime toward which he traveled would be as satisfying as this—no sun's heat, no water's warmth, no breeze's touch. It was like the relief of a pressure he had not fathomed until it was lifted—a nerve unpinned. He had not sensed this peace even before he was exiled at fourteen. Never.

Lawrence swallowed.

There was no going back. There was no possibility of existing outside this mistake. He would live and die with it; if it took forty years, he would—if it took, as it had, four days.

★ ★ ★

Aᴛᴛᴇʀ ʜɪs ᴏʀɪɢɪɴᴀʟ ᴜɴᴡɪʟʟɪɴɢ ʙᴀɴɪsʜᴍᴇɴᴛ, things happened that desocialized him further—an embarrassment, a scare, a set of shocking losses.

Once, when he was twenty, he was humiliated, physically assaulted in front of his closest friends by a group of football fans, fresh from a defeat, who thought he'd said something derogatory of them; another time, when he was twenty-one, he was plagued for months by dire lab tests that were mistakenly attributed to his blood.

These things made him gun-shy, shell-shocked.

Then choice after choice had gone badly. The first career, a banker, was chosen unimaginatively, to please his father; he'd been discharged at twenty-two; the second career, a painter, was chosen rashly, to please himself; he'd been dismissed at twenty-three; the third and present career, a bookkeeper, was chosen for him, by circumstances. He was twenty-four, and it was the only thing left that anyone would let him do. From then on, he'd tallied figures and moved them from screen to screen, balancing and weighing, drawing lines and creating charts. He'd learned that safety, by and large, was a matter of insularity; things stopped happening to him, both for good and for ill.

Then came the deaths of his parents, within a month of each other—one by stroke, one by clot. These drove him into an interior part of himself, like one seeking shelter from falling shrapnel, exploding fire play.

Worst of all, whenever he drew close to intimacy with someone, a panic of exposure flew over him. It was as though at any moment he would sprout gills, horns. The very nearness of another might cause a kind of involuntary revelation of what he was. Their ignorance was his only refuge; his distance, the only means to ensure it.

At length it was as though he was on an island, always in night, but within earshot of another shore. He could hear them, the living, as they toiled and played in sounds that crossed the waves on dark winds; at times he could even make out diffused figures through the shadows as he watched from his moated circlet. He saw them seek each other, caress or rebuff each other, walk hand in hand or turn, back to back.

At other times he felt as though he were inside a diving bell, floating about in the dark night of another atmosphere, a chaos in which others dwelt with elegance and equipoise.

★ ★ ★

THE CHILD WAS THE KEY. He would have to encourage her to keep contact with him, while at the same time never letting the woman know what was happening. He could not scare them, risk having them take themselves away. Still, he had to remain close. There was no choice. He quickly canceled his reservation at the villa and followed them to the baggage claim.

When they got into a cab, he pretended that they were with him. The taxi driver was instructed to stay behind the car that they'd taken, then stop when it pulled into a hotel. At the desk, he stood close enough to hear the woman's name as she gave it to the manager, close enough to hear her confirm her address.

"And what's *your* name?" asked the manager to the child.

Close enough to hear it all, stood Lawrence. Close enough to remember and write it down.

When he learned which floor they were on, he requested the same. He noted their room number, and for the next four days, listened for the sound of its door, opening. When they left, he would also—not exactly with them, but soon after. And from then on, his only occupation was in finding a way to stay within an arm's length or a voice's call.

It was as though he were inserting himself into a picture, placing himself within the background of a portrait others had planned and paid for. The skill lay in never letting them know he was there; he would appear, later, when the shot was viewed, when the coincidence was noticed—a man, materializing, again and again and again.

His joys would be momentary, fleeting. He was unlikely to experience the prolonged ecstasy he'd felt on the flight; those circumstances were too difficult to recreate. But when a stranger saw them, when he mistook the three as belonging to each other; for that instant he, Lawrence, would be part of that stranger's seeing, part of his knowing what a man with wife and child looked like—what they were. If only that simple thing, that men and their wives and their children can be passed, noticed, or ignored—but still part of the universe, like air and water and stars to sleep under—if he was no more than that to the stranger who saw, it was more than he, Lawrence, had ever been party to.

Of course, on one level, it would be a mistake; but on another it would be quite true—just as the heat from a lamp might make a man believe he is warmed by the sun. He can go on believing such a thing forever—with no one to correct him, with no one to care to.

★ ★ ★

O N THE SECOND DAY, the child brought her mother a cup of
orange juice. The girl had taken it from the al fresco buffet,
clutching the glass tightly with both hands, but still sloshing it
onto the terrace tiles for all her pains.

The woman did not smile when it was placed on the table;
she was not looking really. She was preoccupied; her eyes darted
about as though she were trying to find someone. The cloth bag
from the day before lay on the table beside her. Her left hand
rested atop it.

They were having breakfast in the restaurant's patio area, near
a large, lushly decorated pool with palm trees and bougainvillea
and waterfalls spilling from a variety of cantilevered stones.
Lawrence sat nearby, a few tables away, turned at an angle so that
he would not be noticed as he watched.

The mother was on some errand, it was plain to see—
something furtive, perhaps illegal—and took little notice of what
was going on around her. Rather, she was obsessively concerned
with a document in the bag, opening to check for it every few
moments, taking out the envelope itself, undoing the metal clasp
and peering inside to make sure the contents were still there.
From what Lawrence could tell, she was killing time until she
was to meet somebody about this document. Her anxiety had
likely prompted her to fly to the island early, days early, in case
something went wrong.

Later, as they walked about the colonnades and plazas,
dipping in an out of the shops of the nearby streets, the child stayed
close to the woman. It was as though she sensed she would have
to keep an eye on her, to make sure the mother did not lose her.

Perhaps that was how it always was between them, Lawrence
gathered; though an infant, she was nevertheless aware that she was
not being cared for properly. She all but held on to her mother's

hem, drawing on a sense of self-preservation beyond her years. Most of the time, the woman seemed no more conscious of her than a tree is of a vine.

But because of this, Lawrence could stay nearby. Because of this, he could be mistaken as belonging to them, they to him.

In the afternoon, he sat on the side of the pool, his legs dangling beneath the dazzling water. The child played among a set of children sloshing about in the shallow end. The group had a plastic shark of some type, one that sailed through the water with a torpedo's strength. Once, it went astray and bumped Lawrence's leg. He laughed and sailed it back to the girl, who took no more notice of him than if the wind had returned it. Still, Lawrence was satisfied and proud of the exchange.

But what provided him with the pleasure he sought were the pictures, the ones that the parents of the other children took—of all of them playing together in the pool, with Lawrence in the background.

Who is that? Someone might ask, months later, looking at the digitized memory.

A shrug. *One of the fathers, I suppose.*

★ ★ ★

THE NEXT DAY, as the mother was on her phone, arguing wildly with someone as she held the cloth bag under her arm, Lawrence watched the girl.

She played on the terrace lawn near the pool with the same set of children as before. Except this time they were running about in a game that involved a plastic purple streamer. When any one of the children was touched with it, he would freeze, remaining that way until the bearer of the magic ran by and unfroze him with another grazing tap from the streamer. It seemed to have the power to imprison and to liberate, to capture and to free. And once freed, the child danced about in dervish raptures until he was spellbound again by the streamer, which came and went as a comet, trailing its tail in majesty.

There were no more rules than these, from what Lawrence could tell, and yet the children were captivated by the idea. Ten, twenty, then thirty minutes passed.

Lawrence sat on a bench, watching; other parents lay at the pool, some checking in from time to time. Occasionally, one would nod and smile, which Lawrence returned, pleasantly.

Once, when his girl froze in place, she was turned in his direction.

Her small black eyes fell upon him, or at a place near enough to seem so. In that brief time, her gaze drove through him, transfixed him upon the clear plane of being against which he lived, a limbo of presence and weightlessness that, for all its uncertainty, swamped him with both longing and belonging, both call and answer, need and fill.

As he luxuriated in this state, someone approached him, a photographer from the hotel.

"For the brochure," he told Lawrence, when asked.

Lawrence smiled, looked back to the group; the girl was unfrozen now; she gamboled about the grass, her joy as pure and light as a fragrance.

"Just sit there," the photographer said to Lawrence, adjusting his camera lens.

"These your kids?"

Lawrence nodded; the picture was taken. A chronicle— formal, official, undeniable in the impressions it would create in any that ever beheld it.

★ ★ ★

THE THIRD DAY THEY WENT to the theater; Lawrence overheard their plans and went too.

It was raining in soft broken showers that wept and fled and wept again. The rutilant cast of the clouded sun lent the atmosphere the sense of a young girl caught in her moods, unsure of what to trust.

He was surprised, pleased, to find the woman had managed to unburden her mind from her worries enough to plan something nice for the child.

It isn't right, thought Lawrence.

Regardless of what she was worried about, to let every waking moment consume her wasn't right—not when it caused the girl to worry herself. That very morning, at breakfast, he had seen the way the child caught her mother's concern like a cold; it dampened her spirits and spoiled her appetite. The woman should know better; she deserved to be told if she didn't.

But then a waitress had appeared, a large woman with a broad, smiling face. She had given the girl some paper and crayons. And the little gesture, coming when it had, broke the girl from her despair, setting her upon a task of coloring the white spaces red, blue, yellow, and green in a fury of joy-seeking. Even the woman seemed to brighten at the change.

Lawrence had watched; made note.

He followed them at a distance as they walked through the damp street, shielding his face with a newspaper as he trailed. The memory of the change that had come in the morning, that had precipitated this little excursion that the girl was clearly enjoying—skipping and hopping beside her mother as they walked—gave him an idea.

He decided to overtake them, to push ahead and reach the line first. He chose his place carefully, five or six people in between.

Of the three films offered, only one was for children, so he took his chance and said its name.

"Three," he told the ticket seller, paying the price. "Two adults and one child."

Three red tickets, joined in perforation, rose from the machine, like a dry tongue in hope of water; Lawrence received them, tore one off, handed the other two back.

"For them," he said, motioning behind him with a jerk of his head. "The woman in yellow, holding the girl's hand. Give them to her. Tell her it's taken care of, say it's a prize, a special, anything, but don't say it was me."

The ticket seller nodded, unperturbed, as though such a deed were common.

Whatever confusion he was creating, whether they accepted or rejected the offer, Lawrence did not want to witness. So he hurried away, found the right theater, seated himself in the far back corner, and waited.

To his surprise, no one was there but him. He only noticed when he was in his seat, when his eyes had accustomed themselves to the shadows of the vacant space. All at once he felt as though he'd stumbled into an error.

And in the pressure of the darkness, in the silence of the half-drained world, he felt the return of the separating, insulating forces that had jailed him since he was first polluted with their name. They crept beneath his skin in a vengeful wickedness, the retributive rage of a returning tyrant punishing his insolent slaves, those who had sloughed their meek state in his absence, had tested their atrophied limbs, raised their downcast eyes. The awfulness made it seem as though at any moment the force would manifest, present its shaggy head from beneath the velvet veil.

But before he saw its face, before the black moat was pierced by some power strong enough to fetch, the door behind him opened. A blade of dispelling light fell across the room.

In they came, hand in hand; down they sat, side by side; and he, close, so close, that whatever holy rule lay about their togetherness drew him within it; for the time being, he had a place to be, and the music began.

★ ★ ★

THE RAIN CLEARED BY THE TIME they left the theater; the sun was lazy in the island sky, as though it were leaning back into the dusk, falling in a sweep, so that what light it threw against the horizon was the last arch of its reclining.

People took advantage of the balmy few hours left to them, unbridled from their rainy confinement at last. They headed to the beach, to the shops. The woman let the girl jump into the pool as she took up her worries once more, calling different numbers on her phone, raising her hand to the heavens as she spoke.

And Lawrence took up his post on a sun chair, with the other parents, watching.

"How are you?" said a young man, ten years his junior, sitting next to him.

"Fine."

The man extended his hand.

"Jim," he said.

"Lawrence."

"That one there?" he asked, pointing to Lawrence's child.

Lawrence took the question to mean "did she belong to him?" He nodded.

"I thought so. Sorry, but I have to ask. Where'd you get that ladybug float she's on? My daughter's dying to have one."

Lawrence considered what a man posed with such a question would say.

"You'd have to ask my wife. I don't have any idea."

The young man smiled, shrugged.

"I know. I never do either. But it seems like whatever I get for them is just fine for about five minutes, and when they get with some other kids, it stops being fine."

Lawrence laughed, shook his head.

"It won't get any easier."

It all came so effortlessly to him; what to think; what to say. The role was so natural.

"No," said the young man. "At least right now it's just a five dollar pool toy."

"Clothes," said Lawrence, "cars."

"I don't even want to think about it," said the other, feigning horror. "All in due time. 'Sufficient to the day is the evil thereof.'"

Lawrence nodded again. For a while, the two of them sat, shoulder to shoulder in a shared world of cares, responsibilities, plans, futures.

But after a time, it began to bother him. He looked over at the woman, still arguing on the phone, the bag clutched tightly as ever, as though it were all that stood between her and death.

The girl clambered from the pool, soaking wet, and ran by him, laughing.

Clothes, thought Lawrence. Cars.

★ ★ ★

F OR MY DAUGHTER," he said to the agent the next day, "and
my wife."

He took out a policy in his name, with the woman and
child listed as beneficiary, using the address he'd written down
three days ago.

He spoke to his banker as well, to make similar arrangements.
A vast sum that he'd never known what to do with now had a place.
The thought of it escheating to the state had always embarrassed
and sickened him. What was once a profligate waste would now
be a boon, a spring broken from parched ground. Whatever the
cloth bag had meant to them, whatever it did mean, would be
less important now.

On the way back to the hotel, he went to shops, bought
things and had their names printed on them—monograms,
embossments, embroidery.

"I'll pick them up later," he told the storekeepers, "when
we're ready to leave."

He went to church and lit candles, made reservations in
their names, practiced for conversations he would be required
to have in the future:

Three for dinner, he would say. And, *We'd like to look at the
property.*

*I married in my old age, a woman too young—too good—for
the likes of me.*

The grace of a late child. Ah, but what grace.

*Yes, yes, we are all alike in the end, when it comes to those that
we—for whom we . . .*

Well, we are all alike in the end.

★ ★ ★

I T WAS THIS; it was the thought that in the days of devastation, when the universe imploded upon itself in a great fiery undoing, he would be locked inside a closet—neither punished nor blessed, but forgotten, too insignificant to either damn or save, with only his despair as bedmate, choking out voiceless cries that no one would ever care to hear.

★ ★ ★

T HAT LAST DAY he saw her from the beach—far out in the pounding surf, under the roaring sun—too far out.

His heart leapt, broke and rained. He felt himself collapsing like a puzzle, destroyed in frustration.

The day was fierce, with typhoon winds blowing beneath a glorious sky, all crystals and diamonds exploding upon the bright blue field above.

But she was too far out, atop her little float.

While his back was turned, while he was thinking of new ways to follow, to grow near, to remain a satellite revolving about the heat and pull of that which was greater than itself, that made whatever was of worth about itself possible—when his back was turned, she had slipped away, been carried out beyond the breakers to a point that only the color of her suit, the cap of her hair, the shape of her float, could be seen.

Those on the beach had all noticed—other parents with watchful eyes—all pointing, crying out to her, "Too far. Too far."

The lifeguards were nowhere to be found; her mother was nowhere to be seen.

Come back! Come back! Undertow! Riptide! Come back!

But she could not hear over the roar of the wind and the surf, and the brilliant sky laughing.

To have told him he could not swim out would have been to tell him he could never take breath again, could never sleep or swallow. To have told him that the loss of her was something he could bear, overcome—that she was a child who did not, and had not ever, belonged to him, and that he would be the same man after she was lost as he had been before he'd seen her, would have seemed to him the lies of the beast, the mouthings of the wicked thing in the black recess who had shut him up within the dungeon of his skin. The sea was not strong enough to tell him what he could and could not do.

Water about his knees, about his waist, about his head, foaming as he thrashed against what thrashed against him, what threw itself at him in the fury of recoil—lies, that the sea told—lies, all.

With vicious strength he stroked on—strike, strike, gasp and strike.

And in that moment of blue and black frenzy, seawater effervescing about his body, the vacuum of his self at its lowest, his object at its height—he knew that, like a pole on a magnet, there was a pole opposite him. He knew it as sure as he had always known what he was not. In an instant, in a split moment of a moment, it could swing upon itself, molt its nothingness in one vast swallow and come out whole on the other side. It could.

He tore at the water until his legs began to sink, until he stood upright in the fathomless depths more than he floated upon them. With will and defiance, he pulled himself across and over the remaining waves, nearing her as though he were drawing in a rope, hand over hand.

The child seemed to know him as he approached; she was not in danger, was not afraid; she even appeared to recognize him—even seemed to acknowledge his mistake, to pity and have mercy on it.

As for Lawrence, there was no time to realize the unimportant fact that this was not his child at all; that his child was further down the beach, playing in the sand, in a similar suit, but well and safe and complete.

He did not see that irrelevant thing as the water entered his eyes, as the first drink of his coming death slid down his throat, as he shouted through the rapture that exploded in his darkening brain:

"I've had everything. I have everything."

What They Left

ACH CALL STOOD OUT from the next: a soft moan, a low horn, rising. The man's head lifted an inch. His eyes wrinkled at the corners. His tongue touched the top of his palate, as if he smelled fire.

There was nothing to keep him from his work except these sounds, and even they only made him pause for a moment—turn small, keen eyes toward the line of hills, colored black in the last orange light, from which the sounds seemed to come. Then he returned to his labor. A penlight hung from the raised hood of a car's engine, where his hands—the knuckles scabbed and some bleeding—toiled inside the motor. His flesh was raw and cracked and chapped from too much wind, too much weather without gloves, too little idleness.

He had lived past his middle age at the end of this tree-lined road. He had cut the way himself, a narrow alley leading from his back door, through the rear of his property, and ending at his store on the highway. There he sold old things, used things, gathered together by function, then by size, then by cost. Besides him, the only people that used the road were those who abandoned things alongside it. He did not know when it had become a castaway point, but it had happened slowly, and he had noticed it, slowly. After a time, as he made his way home, he began to find iceboxes, dishwashers, gates, air conditioners, lengths of fence, rolls of barbed wire. In the end, weeds took them.

Sometimes he would stop to see if he wanted any of the discarded things for himself—to salvage, reclaim, sell. If anything could be saved, he would slip back at night with a pulley and tackle, winch it against a tree, then slide what he wanted up from the ditch. Sometimes people got there before him, so he had to work fast. Other times people took back what they had left. Once, at his store, a man claimed a tiller that had taken three days to fix:

"This is mine," the man had said, his eyes bright, sharp. "I can tell."

He shook his head, widened his stance so that his body stood at an angle to the other.

"I found it on the road."

"It's mine."

"Not now."

The man had placed his hand on the plastic grip, leaned over the top of the thing, glared: "You stole it. Prove you didn't."

So he had learned. He had to be careful of what he touched. He had to change things, just enough.

This time, though, they had worked too quickly, had been interrupted. He himself might have surprised them, coming down the road. He was thin, but tall, so his feet hit the earth hard and loud as he walked, grinding in the chert. They could have heard him a long way off. Nothing else accounted for how much they had left. The stereo had been slipped out, and some of the engine broken free, but he could work with what remained. It lay, piece by piece, cupped inside his hands; cold and slick and greasy; with his tools, it could be made to tick and turn warm.

It was only a day or so there; not even that. It had come to his notice that morning, as he had walked to work. He might have overlooked it, had not the first of the sun picked out lights in the black paint. The car had been left off the shoulder, down a bank and beside a stand of pines.

His wrench slid over a bolt deep beneath the battery plate. It was a tight fit, but it caught the bolt's angles. After several yanks, the wrench fell into the familiar release and give of loosening. If all went well, the engine would start soon, with new plugs and a new fan for the radiator. He would have to decide what to do with it then, though. The law would come into play. He could not say how, but he would have to decide.

His cap made his head hot. He pulled his hands out of the body and pushed his hat's bill back from his brow. He thought for a moment and ran his fingers over whiskers, three days grown. He raked them back and forth. The bite warmed his face.

There was more to do, but not now. In the morning, then.

It was a small climb up from the stash of trees back to the road. He picked up a bucket of greasy tools, held the light between his teeth, and clawed at the grass with his free hand to keep his purchase. Once there, he took the light from his mouth and shined it in the direction he would take. The beam bobbed before him as he walked—a soft, collapsing tunnel through the dark. The tools jangled in the bucket.

The sounds returned: Two. Three. Silence.

He marched on through three more calls, and rests, and calls, before he stopped and spun toward them, swiveling on his down heel. He stared into the woods for a moment—a gray, ashen blue—then commenced to walk. He kept up the same stride as before, but with the hills facing.

There was no point going on until his mind was free. They might have come back—keys in hand. And he would not surrender his work to theirs. It was no more theirs than his.

He stopped to glance back at the car, then slowly ran his light down its length, fender to bumper, marking the body.

It was almost lost in the dark, now. It would take a man with a light, now.

To find the sounds he would have to crawl down the opposite bank, which fell off at a stiff grade. The light and the bucket together would be too much to carry. He would need a free hand to compensate, so he set the bucket down and drew out a hammer by its claw. He hefted it twice, then once more—once for each sound he had heard—and sat himself on the bank's edge. He went belly first, sliding, the damp ground pressing through his clothes, kissing at his skin.

Now, the only dealings he had with men were with those who came for reclaimed things, gathered by function, size, cost. They found what they wanted, paid or refused the price, then went their way. If he could have left a jar for them to put the money in, he would not have walked down the road every day to watch it happen. But that much, the press of their money on his hand, he had to take. Five years stood between him and his father's death, the last man he had to take more from or of. Twisted by strokes, his body hunched to the side, one arm useless, the old man had died in his own bathwater and been buried in land filled with strangers. He had thought at the time that dying was the last of a man's cost. He knew better now.

His grip tightened around the hammer. The last man he had lived with he had seen dead; and now the next he would see living, he would make dead.

Near the bottom of the bank, he turned onto his back, took to his feet, brushed himself off. Ahead were shallow woods, and on the other side of the woods, a field. The light was not as strong as it had been, so he snapped off the switch to save the battery.

His eyes adjusted for a moment, then he felt through the dark by the violet paper sky.

The sounds, three, came again as he edged onward; he could tell their direction better. He was not afraid.

On the other side, a field of harvested corn stretched before him, running half a mile toward the hills. Months had passed since the picker had been here; the place looked raked and ripped, the shorn stalks rotten from rain, wind. He held the hammer against the back of his right thigh and shined the light along the corn, looking for what he expected.

Water, or dew, or blood, glistened along the girl's legs. He could not tell if she had lost part of one limb from the knee down, since only her left side was visible. The right leg might be tucked beneath her. He craned his neck to get a better view, but could see only a thrashed-out spot in the stalks, a place lain in so long it had become a trap.

Dragged herself from the woods, he decided. They had dumped her there, then returned to the car at the road. Little by little, she had crawled, passing out and coming to.

The girl made the sounds again, low moans into the earth beneath her face. That had caused them to sound as they had. Other than hers, there was no noise. No one else was there.

He eased the light about her body in an arc. But as the beam reached her head, she began to turn in his direction, as if he had spoken. Her lips made a dry, smacking noise.

"John," she murmured, her eyes bleary. It might have been a question.

Before she could say it again, he pressed through the ragged corn, clattering about him like laughter. He drew his boot back and drove the steel toe up beneath her ribs. She gave, her body lifting, then sinking onto the top of his foot. He paused, set to do it again, but she fell quiet and still. He yanked his boot from beneath her settling weight.

Night was full on him; in the few moments it had taken to see and know what she was, the sky had darkened. It was not entirely black. There would be stars. But the air was sharp. It had grown darts and picked at his skin and lungs.

He could not keep the car now. The simple news came all of a piece, unquestioned, unimpeachable. She belonged to the car, and whatever they had done to her, it had not been enough. And if he finished the work he had started, the law would figure further than he could see to the end of.

He shined his light down at the hammer: black and blue and cold, an old hammer, his father's hammer. The wood was bleached from the sun—from hand oil—from years of fixing things.

If he left the car where it was, they might find it, then find her, then find him. He was the only man anywhere near this place. And, too, he had touched the car. He had doctored it just enough, so that someone could tell. They had left too much.

The girl stirred, her shoulder blades twitching. With a turn of his light, he took her length.

She had both legs after all. One was only crumpled beneath the other, not lost. Still, it was broken. A blue-white bruise swelled from below and behind the knee. By her even skin, he could see she was young—fourteen, fifteen. But she was not dressed for the weather, in a short, black jacket, a white skirt hiked up around the top of her thighs. She bled from somewhere around her waist. A dried rivulet ran along her broken leg.

He moved the light to her head. Her short hair was both blonde and black and was pushed toward her face. Another rivulet ran across her temple and bloodied her cheek. He stepped closer, squatted, and shined the beam onto the top of her head. A wedge had been rent in her scalp, parting the hair in a zigzag.

He cut the light off and sat back on the ground.

If he picked her up? She might die on the way. He could not carry the light and the hammer and the girl. He looked across the field.

A fence separated it from another stretch of land—one his father had grown tobacco on, and shot a man's hog on—a slug through the belly, so it would drag itself home to die. The road lay beyond that.

She might die before he got her there, or even then, before a car came along. If he left her and went to the road himself, she might also die. It was too cold now, and would be colder yet; too cold to live with a wedge cut out of her head, and bleeding from the waist. She should not have lived as long as she had.

He closed his eyes. What would the law say, with him standing on a road in the night, holding a dead girl, her car nearly fixed? Nothing came to him. He could not see that far.

He switched on the light again, its beam falling before his eyes—a stepping-down color, setting and settling, warmer as it died—more gold than yellow. The glow would not last long enough for him to make up his mind.

It was better to leave some mark, to show that he had tried. Something had to be left, to testify. He placed the light on the ground, aimed away from her eyes so that he could see, but not wake her. He stood again, unzipped his coveralls and pulled the legs over his boots. Now he was only in his pants and shirt, and the cold crept up his spine and down his collar.

He sank to his knees and crawled toward the girl. With the light aimed at her shoulders, he laid the coveralls, warm from his own heat, on top of her. The cloth spread from one bone cap to the other, with enough to lie on the ground at both sides.

How small she was; how small. She could not be this small and live in this cold dark.

He placed the rest on top of her waist, her hips, her thighs, her calves—his body matching hers, overwhelming hers. Finished, he rocked back on his knees.

She had not moaned or moved in a long while. A cold, quiet moment passed as he felt for the light. Slowly, he shined what was left of its power into her face.

Her teeth glistened first, then the sparks in her open eyes. She watched him with a long fathomless look. There was warmth behind it, not the abandoned gape of his father, slumped dead in his bath. Her lips quivered.

He scrambled back. "Hey," he said and nudged her thigh with his hand. "Hey."

She would not answer. Her lids were shut partly, but the wits were now asleep again.

She could not have seen him; not his face, at least. It was too dark. And the light had been in her eyes. She was too dazed to recall him, even if she had seen.

Still. Still. And she had said what she had said. And he had done what he had done.

They were leaving more and more, like a bad trick. The car, then her, and now her memory. If he left her now, she might come to altogether. After all, his father had, many times, come back. Maybe she would come to, stumble up, walk to the road; she might never see the marks he had left. She might remember only his face and nothing more. The last thing is always what you remember.

He would have to give her some other thing to remember last. He could see that far.

★ ★ ★

Y OU SELL CAR PARTS, and shit like that?" the policeman had asked. He leaned against the iron post that held up the front porch. "That's right."

"You own that junk stand? Up there on the road?"

He was fat and sweaty and smelled of green aftershave. He chewed stick after stick of gum. Another policeman, bony, with a mustache as thin as a boy's, sat on the front step. He dug dog shit from the soles of his patent leather shoes with a piece of tree bark.

"I sell parts," he had answered.

"Must be doing pretty good, if you're this busy," the fat one said.

"It's never too good."

"Well, must be. You were there instead of here."

He unwrapped the foil from a white stick of gum—spearmint— and shoved it into his full mouth. "Why'd you leave him, in the state he was in?"

"I have to work."

The fat man frowned, squinted. "He stays—stayed—here while you were at work?"

"Yes."

"You couldn't get nobody to stay with him? In the state he's in?"

"No."

The man popped his gum. "How long did he stay alone?"

"'Til I got done."

"All day, then?"

"'Til I got done."

He looked over the policeman's shoulder, through the open front door to the place where his father lay. They had put newspapers over his face and crotch, the sheaves wilting from the damp. The rest of him lay in a puddle made from bathwater that dripped from his body. He seemed more twisted than he had when alive.

"Didn't you think something might happen to him?"

"Nothing ever did."

The man nodded. "Something always happens. Eventually."

"Never did before."

He grunted out a little laugh. "You left him in the bathwater?"

"Yeah. Half of him didn't work good, but he could move around for himself."

"Well, not good enough. He couldn't get out."

"He always could before. He—"

"Well, he couldn't this time."

"Shit!" the other man yelled as his stick broke. He got up, stormed into the yard, and snapped a shoot from a tree branch. Then he came back, sat down, and began to dig again, scraping the brown paste off onto the porch's edge. The other watched for a while.

"You didn't leave him any way to get in touch with you?" he continued. "You didn't try to get in touch with him during the day?"

"I didn't have anything to say to him. He didn't have anything to say to me."

"Well, I guess he did this time. Since he couldn't get out." He moved closer, jabbed him in the chest with his middle finger. "You don't seem to understand. You let him freeze."

It took a moment to grasp. "I didn't."

The fat man drew back with an amazed look on his face.

"Don't see how you can very well say that. Don't see nothing that says otherwise. Just an old man, froze dead in his bathwater." He looked at the other man on the step: "You see anything else, Mitchell?"

The little man threw the stick, end over end, into the yard.

"All I see's dog shit."

★ ★ ★

H E TOOK THE COVERALLS from her body and laid them out like a blanket. Then he lifted her on top of them, crossed her arms over her stomach, and placed his own arms beneath her shoulders and knees.

You could not be anywhere near, he had thought to himself, time and again. But now, despite himself, he was made to. All he had wanted was the car.

He listened for a moment, to hear if his touch would make her speak. If she spoke again—if she said that again—he would not be able to touch her. His fingers moved around to find a ledge on her body.

They left it all up and down the road, whatever they could not burn or bury. Sometimes you could ignore them. But sometimes they left something you wanted. And once you reached and caught hold, you wound up drawing back more than you meant. From then on, it was hard to tell. You could speculate, guess—but not tell.

She was so light that he used too much heft to lift her from the ground. He nearly lost his grip as he rose. His fingers clutched tight, but he had to hold her so that she was practically square against his chest and stomach, hers pressed to his.

At the movement, she let out a long groan, a yowl. Her leg twisted at a wild angle, like a coat hanger bent by a mad child.

His shirt was wet from frost that lay over her in a spray. How could she be so wet, so soon?

He stumbled forward, without the hammer, without the light.

★ ★ ★

M UST NOT HAVE LIKED HIM MUCH," the little man said, digging in the other sole now. He kept his gaze down.

"What difference does that make?"

"Unh-hunh. Didn't then?"

"What do you care?" His voice was louder than he meant for it to be.

"Now. I see," said the fat one. He stretched his gum in a web over his tongue. It was white and red, like a chicken's skin. "If it was my Daddy—"

"Well, it wasn't. It was mine."

"Unh-hunh," he smiled. "Didn't mean much to you, then."

He shook his head, again, too hard, too fast. "He meant what he meant. He—"

"Unh-hunh. Justa old man, then. Crippled?"

"No. My daddy. And—"

"There he was, calling—" the little one broke in, soft, as though he were in the presence of a sleeping child.

"You don't know that."

The fat man popped his gun.

"Neither do you. Seems to me you—"

"I didn't. Why do you want to say that?"

"You might as well have."

He stepped back, sideways to them both.

"I might as well have, seeing as how this is all gonna play out."

The man smiled. "You don't have any idea how it's all gonna play out."

He was going to answer that. He had meant to answer that.

★ ★ ★

H E MADE IT TO THE END of the first field before stopping
to rest. He would have to think how to get her over the
fence. The wounds had frozen sealed, but if he dropped her over
the top of the page wire, like a calf, her leg might split open, or
her head might give way.

He laid her on the ground beside the fence, then felt the
cold air skate against his chest. She had kept it warm, though
she had seemed very cold while he carried her.

His eyes used to the dark, he found where the wire joined
the top post. Both were old, the wire and the post. His father
had put them in: cedar, wire, staples. He used one hand to hold
the top steady, the other to grip the wire. Then he scotched the
bottom with his boot. After three good pulls, the staple came
loose. He did the same all the way down the measure of the post,
then placed his sole on the top of the wire and crushed it down
with his foot. Once he had the girl in his arms again, across his
chest, he stepped over into the field.

You could not run from them. And they never really threw
anything away; not really. Nothing was done with, once and for
all. If you fixed it, if you just brushed it with your skin . . .

The road was only a hundred yards away. But there should
have been cows in this pasture—Holstein, with white patches
that would glow on a starry night. He could not see or hear or
smell them as he staggered across ground that crunched with a
new coldness. Someone had changed what he remembered, too
much for him to recognize it anymore. For a moment, he was
unsure which way the road lay.

He stopped and turned his head, trying to feel with his face,
to find a place that smelled of open asphalt. Finally. It was where
it should have been.

He would be at the road soon, he thought, walking. He could set this down soon. But then something jerked at his mind, a rough hand inside his head.

Even if it looked right to him, who was to say it would look right to the next? It could take years explaining, years ending, if it ever ended at all, if it could ever be explained. He knew it could. It had before.

He looked down at the girl, wrapped in his clothes. Her head bobbed roughly as he walked through the field. She might have stirred in his grip. He thought she had, but his arms were asleep for the most part, and he could not tell if the throb he felt was the blood dying in his limbs or hers.

All at once he lurched forward. The field fell off at a low spot, and he began to stamp wildly about the pavement. The clapping sounds stung like pistol shots.

Feeling through the dark with his feet, he had not realized he was so close to the road. He had expected another fence, another thing to have to lift her over, but what he remembered had been pulled down. His back strained under the pull as he stumbled about. He planted his steps wide, to keep his base, then tossed the girl up high on his chest. He stopped to catch his breath, his balance regained.

The pavement was silver and blue, somehow softer than the ground. He stared down one direction, then turned and stared down the other.

Should he wait here or keep walking? Which way, if he walked, should he go? If they looked behind what they saw, without someone to tell them what to see?

He edged to the right a few steps. But before he could get far, the crooks of his arms cramped, hitching for lack of blood.

She had become a shadow in his arms. She lifted her head, mumbled, but still a shadow. He could feel her voice coming from a shade within a shade.

When she spoke this time, sense would be strung through the words, threatening like a thing stirred from his own chest, harvested deep from his own throat.

John.

He looked at where her face would be.

"You say my name again, and I'll drop you in this road. You say that again, and the first car comes along, you go under it. You say that again . . ."

★ ★ ★

JOHN, OLE BUDDY. Doesn't look good. Gonna have to make a call."

"Who to?"

The man had laughed. "You'll see."

"For what?"

"You'll see. John, you don't just let an old man—"

"I didn't."

"How you know you didn't?"

He had stood there, staring.

"Well, there you go," the man said.

★ ★ ★

WHO'RE YOU TALKING TO? Who're you calling at?"

He was cold from sweat, surprised at how wet he felt. For all he knew, he was wet from her. In the dark, as he carried her, as she said what she said, the whole time she could have been dressing him in her blood. He had meant to leave a mark, to show them how to see it. But instead, she had left one. And that would be the testimony. That was what they would see. Even if she were to say it again, even if she were saying it now, he would be unable to stop her.

His head felt light. He swallowed in a dry, spitless way.

It was too large to see, too large and dark to get your eyes around or through. You needed somebody else to say, from some high place, that he saw what you did. Otherwise, they might make up what they wanted: "How'd she get there? How'd you come across her? Can anybody account for where you were? What you said? What were you after, anyhow?"

Light approached, though he had not heard it coming down the long, straight way. He did not move aside, but stood firm on the earth, a vague flatness against which she held them.

The beams grew, separated. There came a deepening sound, like sand poured into a box. With an odd sorrow, he understood the light would move to the side, pull next to him.

It slowed and stopped.

Beautiful. Black, smooth, purring with a hot, slick life. All he had meant to have.

With a screech that made him start, step back, look down at the girl, the window lowered. Glass squealed against the rubber guard. The silhouette of a man's head. His voice was rough.

"What happened?"

Happened? "I found her."

"Where?"

He looked back toward the field. "Back there."

"Is she alive?"

He gazed down at the black weight.

"She . . . right now, she is."

The voice at the window talked to someone beside him. The two voices grew louder.

One wanted them, one wanted to send someone back. In the end, the man made a disgusted noise. He rose and struggled around to reach the back door latch, then pushed it open.

"Get in, then."

There was no light to help him place her on the back seat, to lay her in a spot so narrow. A moment passed before he could pull his dead limbs loose from her body. As he released and drew back, he sensed how cold he would be.

"Oh no, you don't. Get in. We've got to see about this."

He slid onto the floorboard beside her and pulled the door closed.

The engine fell into gear, climbed into speed.

"Did you carry her far?" the other voice said, a woman's— quiet, scared, fast.

"I don't know."

"Did you ask her what happened?"

"No."

"Did you see it happen?"

"No."

"Were you alone?"

"Yes."

She stopped, turned in her seat. He could not tell if she was looking down on him or had turned away. He could not tell the direction from which she spoke.

"It's good you came along, isn't it?"

She lay above him, at the level of his eyes, as though on a shelf or a table—an offering of some dark function, weight, price.

Wind poured through the window that had not yet been raised—down his collar, across his raw skin. He pulled his knees close, crouched inside the tight shade, and listened to the motor surround him. He felt the gears shift more and more thinly, the metal of the chassis shivering with change. It traveled against the cage of his hips, the span of his bones, each ball, each socket. The whole of the engine ticked and warmed beneath its own power, with him inside, riding above wheels that would travel beyond the limits of his sight.

Native Language

THEY HAD NEVER EXPECTED HIM to be this good. Harrington himself had never expected it. His students, from the first, thirty-eight years ago, down to the most recent, the class he teaches now, are consistently shocked to have their interests piqued by a lecture on poetry that even he admits has limited value.

Whenever he leaves the room after his class, Harrington's pants are dusted with chalk at the pockets from where he has placed hands on hips while questioning a student: "And what does the author mean by the size of the sun and the height of the moon?" Whenever he leaves the room, his thinning hair is strung with sweat, it too chalked from raking his fingers through his scalp, time and again. Whenever he leaves the room, he is inflamed, galvanized, breathless, but blushing so hard he is faint from the pressure of his blood, and often has to steady himself on the doorframe.

There is no accounting for his powers in ordinary terms; he is not pedantic, or imposing, or counter-cultural. He is small and wiry like a classic, pantalooned pedant; but he has a boyish body frozen in a boy's preadolescent grace. He wears nice clothes, timeless and well tailored, and has sharp, Germanic features that might pass for imposing in another man. But his small green eyes give over too quickly in smiles, and his lips never shut on his teeth. He can create a rebellious air, because at certain moments he seems aloof, at others, electrifying. But this is true only when he speaks on his subject, when he talks about his own particular interest, with its two-hour breadth and one-hundred-fifty-year depth. Otherwise, he is quiet. He never talks at meetings, and because he received tenure thirty-two years ago, skips most of them or feigns sickness to leave others. He lives alone. His wife is dead. He has no children. He has no family either, except for one sister, who idolizes him. She lives only two hours away, but he rarely sees her. He is too embarrassed to see her.

If he could walk out of the class and into his grave, he would. The ecstasy has never been greater than the night of his first triumph, his first class, but it has never slackened either. What has changed is the ever-increasing, and now matched, feeling of shame. It does not come with him into class, but pops up, hot and quick and full-blown, like a demon's face, just as the session ends. A number of things could provoke it: the way the students furiously scribble down or type into laptops some final points he makes; the way others, their mouths open, stare at his drama, delighted with him in spite of hairdos and hair colors and cuts of skirt and piercings of flesh that say they could not care less. The feeling is strong enough that he schemes for ways to exit before any can stop him. But despite his hurry, they always get to the podium in time, and one or two are always effusive. They have never thought of things this way, the way they are thinking now, since him.

"Good! Good!" he says, stuffing books and notes into his briefcase, tearing and crumpling pages in his speed. "I'm glad you like the subject. Yes, that's wonderful. It's a good work. More people should know about it. I . . ."

But then, before he can break into a trot out the door, she says: "No. *You're* the one they should know about. I'm not just saying that to impress you either. *You . . .*"

And when they say these things, he might have turned golden in front of them, like a god in a myth. Frozen, golden, but still able to see inside; cursed, melting with unseen sorrow. Granted, it always fades away, and it stays away until the waning moments of the next evening's class. But then it comes forth resolutely, like the knells of war, like tocsins from an approaching enemy. It is as though he is holding himself out as something glorious, as though by doing a fundamental, involuntary thing, he is crowning himself before them, like a minor Napoleon, staging a public abomination.

But then, he is glorious—at this—and it is impossible for him not to be. Only because he can still somehow manage beneath the coequal weight, neither shoulder nor heart collapsing, can he carry on. Still, it has grown worse lately, more powerful, in each of its component parts—neither present nor absent without the other, each identically strong, and growing stronger.

As the summer semester approaches, Harrington prepares himself. In his head, he scans through his opening comments. The lines are always the same and always effective. He does not particularly care whether the students learn or not, although they always say they do. He prides himself on needing no computer images, handouts, pictures—certainly no films. His colleagues fight over "smart classrooms," those dedicated to the Internet and outfitted with the powers of a planetarium in mid-solstice. But he prefers a room that is designed like an operating theater, ready for a class in surgery techniques. It is almost as remote from the thriving heart of the department as his office—his first and only—located in the pharmacy complex. If it were not for the fact that his mailbox is in the humanities building, his colleagues would never see him.

He thinks that is why the department head has called him over, to once again coax him into the same nest as the others. Why he should still bother is beyond Harrington.

"There you are," says Bradshaw.

He kicks a chair out toward Harrington as he comes through the office door. The man is not unlike Harrington in appearance: the same height and build and narrow features. But he is dour, and wears a shady beard that grows haphazardly and is left unbarbered, like a prisoner's. His clothes have an accidental appearance, clashing in pattern and color. He has a reputation for being both imposing and counter-cultural.

Rather than take the chair to which Bradshaw is pointing with his foot, Harrington moves behind it. He places a hand on the back, licks his lips, grins.

"You can close the door," says Bradshaw.

"Oh no. That won't be necessary, I'm sure."

"It might be, so please do. And have a seat."

"Oh no. I prefer to stand."

Bradshaw gives a shallow sigh that whistles through his teeth. He rises to push the door shut, then sits on the desk.

"Well," he says, "I'll tell you right now you're going to hate this. But there's no way out, and that's that. No way out. None. None. None."

Harrington laughs, his attention already breaking free of the man. He focuses on a set of shelved textbooks, theoretical in calling.

There is, too, a way out; there is, always. He has ignored his way through forty years of dreadful predicaments. He could have walked though Nagasaki in 1945 without a gas mask.

Bradshaw pushes back on the desk and grips the edge. He flexes his knees, alternating each cap so that they bulge like bullfrogs beneath his pants. It seems to give him a needed distraction as he orders Harrington to take a sabbatical.

". . . And that's the way it is. You've never taken one—not ever, as far as anyone can remember. The secretary's been here twenty-six years and she can't recall even *one*. Of course, you predate her and every other secretary and janitor on the campus. But I know you haven't, because I did the research myself. You're past retirement, and you haven't taken one."

"I don't—"

Bradshaw squeezes his knees and his eyes at the same time, as though suffering an electric shock.

"No. No. I have to get through this. I have a lot to do today. I have to lead that committee on recruiting students with Lupus for the new Melanin Studies Program. So I don't have time for a fight. It's all decided. No way out. None."

"I don't want—"

"You've never taken one. And we *have* to take sabbaticals, all of us, or we'll lose the privilege. The school is cracking down on not taking sabbaticals. The people in the sciences are taking them left and right. If we don't keep up, they'll get ours."

Bradshaw pushes on, stirred by his speed and eloquence. Usually, within minutes of a meeting with Harrington, it has ended with Bradshaw alone—refused and dismissed. But today he has stumbled into a groove, bowling the man over, shutting him out utterly, like a blanket, a glass, a fire extinguisher, and a water hose, all used to snuff out a baby's birthday candle. He locks his knees in the fashion of a bridegroom at his wedding, clutches the desk. With eyes shut tight, he blurts out the rest.

"You have to do it this very next semester. It's decided."

Then, in a flash of inspiration, he jumps from the desk, pushing away like a diver from a platform. He speeds through the open door, using Harrington's own escape route against him. He calls behind as he runs: "I have to go! I won't be back! You'll get a letter from the department. See you next year. Goodb—"

Bradshaw does not quite manage the last farewell, as he knocks a girl flat in his haste and trips over her neck. Still, he crabs along the floor to the staircase and fumbles down before Harrington can chase after.

The rest of the afternoon Harrington spends standing behind the chair in Bradshaw's office. He was not telling the truth. He *has* to come back. His phone is ringing off the hook, and the department secretary comes in and out, looking for him. He has to come back, and when he does, Harrington will spit up the sabbatical just as strongly as it has been rammed down his throat. Let one of the new hires take it. He himself will not.

But time passes, and Bradshaw spitefully, treacherously, stays away, leaving Harrington to grow nauseous at the prospect of—a year did he say? An entire year?

For a time, Harrington stays home more. He has not cleaned his house since last Christmas, and that was done only in hopes of selling it. He wants a smaller place, with no grass to mow, but nobody has offered what he demands. It is the kind of small, brick, unimaginative house that people buy to tear down and replace. In fact, all of the others like it have suffered that fate; he is a disgrace to the surrounding colonials. When he bought the house all those years ago, he never intended for the neighborhood to come back.

Once the house is clean, he decides to visit his sister, who is ecstatic at the prospect. Her home is large and rich, as she is married to a good-natured doctor who likes Harrington as much as the sister. There is a pool and a country club, right up the hill. They have nice dogs and a big garden. There are two grandsons and four granddaughters who visit often and are remarkably well behaved. It breaks her heart when he says he has to get home to check on his own garden, a lie they both have the sad good taste not to call such.

One night, weeks later, he sits in his green leather club chair, working through all of the novels and poems that he usually teaches. His laptop is at the ready, in case he finds any angles he has not seen before. But at the end of the third work, he realizes, staring at the blinking cursor on his pure white screen, that there are no angles he has not already discovered. He puts his hand out for a fourth work that sits stacked with the others beside his chair, but sighs and draws back.

They are not very good in the first place—the plays, poems, dramas he specializes in. He knows them too well to pretend at new depths. He is like a father who understands the limits of his own son's speed and prowess: "He cannot catch that" . . . "He will not be able to run that fast" . . . "He will lose that one in the sun." He cannot unknow what he knows of their nature. And it is no use adding new works to the list. In his period, they are generally of the same quality; it is the driest in all of literature. Neither could he take on another, more interesting, richer period to occupy himself. He loves what he loves; besides, it is not his gift to teach anything else. Were he to stand then and there, in his house shoes and boxer shorts, trying out Browning or Faulkner or Yeats, he would not be glorious; his exegesis is given to this era alone. He is a vessel of precise use and cannot pretend otherwise. Yet somehow, too, he feels he is a vessel who has never been used in precisely the right way. He has been adored, but never emptied.

He closes his books, turns off his computer, rises. The only thing left to do is teach. No one at the school needs to know.

It takes him about two and a half days to find a class, a group of night students from Latin America, working on bachelor's degrees. The school is new, only two years old. It has already graduated four classes. A great deal of credit, he learns, is given for life experience. If they can type and send e-mails, they are started as sophomores. One woman's heart attack has advanced her a whole year ahead toward a physical therapy certificate. So when he is told that his students are English majors, but that he will have to accommodate their varying degrees of language understanding—that he will have to "meet the students where they are"—he gathers that his lectures will go largely misunderstood, or misapprehended, or not apprehended at all. This is acceptable. A faint hope stirs that he has solved his dilemma.

The extremely busy administrators are housed in space that used to be a travel agency. In fact, many of them had been travel agents. When the school decided to expand with campuses in the suburbs, it recruited the kind of people that could help it achieve its many goals. As a result, there is no campus, per se. Classes are held all over town, at night, in various high schools, gymnasiums, institutional basements, and catastrophe shelters. Harrington's is scheduled for a parochial K-8, attached to a church he knows from baptisms, weddings, the funerals of friends.

Of the eight people in his class, six work at a plant that puts cane bottoms in chairs; the school has a tuition-for-education contract with their employer. All are middle-aged and dressed as though they are headed for a barbecue: T-shirts, cut-off shorts, and flip-flops. The other two are plump, sweet-faced maids at the nearby Holiday Inn, still in their beige, apron-fronted uniforms. Every class, the eight arrive and set their books out before them on the desktops, like plates from which they expect to be served. That is the most that they do with them. And after every class, Harrington locks the door behind him—a duty above all others he has been charged, with seriousness, to observe.

One night, he follows out behind the two maids, deep in earnest conversation, one talking at a furious pace, the other agreeing with extreme approbation. Then, as though they have tagged hands in a hushed, occult moment, they switch places. The other commences talking, accompanied by the brisk, metronomic nods of her companion. He recognizes a theme to their talk: the name "Conchita," said decisively, and the word *"puta,"* said emphatically.

The women walk down a long hall of doors that interrupt vast stretches of wall, each covered with children's art, children's names, children's mysteries. Harrington tracks them, hoping not to be seen, enjoying his anonymity, his stealth. The dark conceals him, makes him feel a student of rare and privy things, a tracker of ancient ways. For in the brilliant fluency of their native tongue, the women might have been two priestesses, two charm-bringers on a mission of great good. The flourishes, the gestures, the trilling of their tongues, suggest that they know their powers, and practice them with trust and hope.

Finally, out the double aluminum doors they go, crossing in front of the church as they head toward the parking lot. Harrington follows behind, listening more than seeing. Their voices roll through the night air with a peculiar lushness, a dark blossoming that unfolds there. He draws closer still, to be engulfed by the fullness of their bloom.

Then they come directly before the front doors of the church, for some reason still open to the vast shadows inside. All at once, both stop talking, stop listening, as abruptly as a needle yanked from a record. Harrington's shoes make a loud scratch on the sidewalk; he jerks himself to a halt. The women do not notice. Instead, each turns her head toward the doorway, crooks a knee, genuflects, bobs up, processes past. They resume their exchange once on the other side—"Conchita . . . *hija de puta*"—and are well toward the lot by the time Harrington can start after.

From then on, every night he follows them. And each night, they do the same thing: stop as though at the mouth of a cave, peer inside to observe a silent obeisance to a hidden source, then begin again once past. Harrington, as he steals close, always searches the dark behind the doors, for what they see or know; but for all he can make out, it is quiet and empty; no service, no lights, no people, no drama. Still, in time, he allows a slight nod to whatever it is.

At the middle of the scheduled twelve weeks he is asked his first question in class. Looking up from his text, he sees that one of the maids has partly raised her hand. How long it has been that way, he is unsure. Harrington smiles and calls her name.

"Señor?" she asks, dropping her arm. She smiles brightly.

"Yes?" He stops in mid-sestina, his book open in one palm. "Go ahead. What is it? Am I talking too fast?"

She shakes her head, then gazes around at the others for encouragement. They all smile and nod her on.

"No. But señor. How you do this? This you do now? How?"

Harrington feels a brief, flushing chill, as though he has stepped on a needle.

Impossible, he thinks.

"How do I do what?"

She blushes harder. "This. This. You are," all at once she throws out an arm and points at him, "*magnifico*, señor! *Magnifico!*"

He steps on several more needles.

"But—"

"*Magnifico! Magnifico!*" a chair-caner echoes. Then, to Harrington's horror, they begin to clap, as if he has just risen from a piano, or taken a violin from his shoulder.

"*Como? Como?*" asks the least literate of the women, shaken by the inexplicable clapping. Her eyes move toward the fire escape.

"*El!*" says another, punching her in the shoulder.

"*Ahhh—Ellll! Si, si, si! Magnifico!*" and she joins the others in applause.

Harrington steps back from their consuming zeal. They look like small children at their first birthday party, taken with everything they see, sure that they have stumbled into a world of brighter spirits and better joys.

Outrageous. In his past two classes, he has not said over eight things they have written down in their spanking new notebooks. He is sure one woman has been making a shopping list the whole semester, and another has been reading Tarot cards. He is defiant that they should look so pleased.

"I don't have anything else to say tonight," he snaps, glancing at the clock on the wall.

Unfortunately, class is not only over, but has been over for ten minutes. His idea of leaving in a mysterious huff is spoiled by his having captivated them well past the end of the session.

All of the classes until the end are the same, a climbing scale of horrible triumphs. He can barely breathe at the finish, at which time they give him a clutch of orange roses and a rainbow-colored piñata. When the school secretary calls to renew his contract, he turns her down flat.

"You can't be serious," she says. "They love you. We love you."

"I'm sorry. I just remembered another commitment. I have a conflict."

"We'll change the time, then. That spot is too late for you—"

"No. No."

"Please. The Hispanics will be destroyed. They're inquiring about the masters program."

"No!"

"More money then. We have so little for English. But what about teaching English as a second language? Bigger classes, more demand, more money. That's how we do things. They're held in the church basement. You—"

He pretends there is a problem with the phone to get rid of her.

Harrington next considers a deaf academy, or a blind one, but is unsure how to go about teaching there. He also suspects his qualifications are unsuitable. Besides, he knows of no such academies in the area, and even if there were, it is doubtful they would need his specialty.

Four months into his hell, it is time to settle things. After his classes with the Spanish, his malady is just as strong. In all likelihood, it would be stronger if he had not been forced into the sabbatical, since his regular students could articulate their compliments much more fully. If things continue on this path, he decides, he will be dead of a stroke by next Christmas term. If he does not teach, he will go insane, or come down with some equivalent of the bends.

In answer, he goes to the hardware store and buys a pair of sliding closet doors to replace the ones in his guest bedroom. A mirror covers the surface of each. Since he has no furniture in the room, other than a bookshelf, he will have no trouble using the area as a studio.

After he installs the doors, he sets up a makeshift podium in front of the mirrors and tests them out. His teaching perimeter will be slightly circumscribed in the smaller room, but all in all, he has enough space to teach at the podium, walk about in front, circle behind to the bookcase, from which he has hung a blackboard, and generally move about as he makes his points. In fact, it may be better, since he can outfit the shelves with many auxiliary texts.

With everything ready, he pulls the plastic off one of his cleaned suits and dresses himself up. He eats a big dinner of chicken-fried steak, a twice-baked potato, a green salad with orange French dressing, a piece of chocolate pie, and drinks a lager of dark beer—all purchased, except for the beer, from the grocery store deli. Finished, he sits still for ten minutes and reads the paper, and when his watch alarm goes off at 6:20 p.m., he rises from the table. With his books under his arm, he sets out for the guest bedroom to test his theory.

"So, there you are," he says, glancing in the mirror at himself glancing at himself behind the podium. The late summer sun seeps through the window sheers and paints the glass with a flat, ashen light.

"Now. Let's begin. The subject for study tonight is the third of the four cantos, with special attention to the fifth and sixth lines of the stanza, where we find an image of the sleeping King David."

The sound of his voice is a bit odd, ringing out the door and down the adjoining hall as it does. But if he moves the podium to the right a few inches, and tilts it just so, his voice will land against the wall and come back to him. He will eat his own echo, as it were.

"You can see David lying on his couch, prostrate from his love, spent from dancing before the ark of God."

He makes a gesture at this point, watching himself recline, buckling at the knees. He squints at his reflection.

He had always held the book in the right hand and let the left arm dangle to the side—this being the image of David in the canto. But when he catches a glimpse of himself in the mirror, the gesture is not as nice as he intended. He switches to the other side, repeating the move, but capturing its negative: the book in his left, dangling the right, buckling the right knee, facing the students—now reduced and collapsed on himself.

Much better. That is more dramatic. More—he smiles at the effect—*magnifico*. In the future, he will have to remember to be the negative of his positive.

For a while, he continues, adjusting his image whenever a new self-discovery is made in the mirrored doors. It seems to work. He can say and do what he loves to say and do, but without the old torturous heave and plunge. The joy is gone, true. Mid-way done, the time at which he would have begun to glow, he feels no particular pleasure. On the other hand, when he is three-fourths done, he feels no particular shame, either. There is no one to fear racing up to the podium, no eyes glistening, no breaths exasperating. He alone is the teacher and he alone the student. On he goes, watching and performing like a two-headed thing. He and his image can bestow no compliment that he or his image does not deserve. Each half cancels the other.

It might, he thinks near the end—a step too far—it might not have happened at all.

Heat rinses through his head.

His image closes the book, the last he sees of it.

Several minutes pass before he can sidle out into the hall, reach back, cut off the light, and close the door. A whole hour passes before he can reenter the room to retrieve the books. Even then, it is with eyes down. The meal he gorged himself upon, though not unusual, does not sit well with him that night. Sleep comes hard. He showers before morning.

The next day he fasts. Then he takes up only bread and water for the two days following. He denies himself television, and makes sure to rise promptly one hour before his alarm so that he can jog around the neighborhood. He hates running more than anything in the world, but while he runs, he is able to think.

At the end of the week he permits himself a bath and a shave, eats a reasonable breakfast, dresses in a navy blue suit, and sits at his kitchen table. At length, he picks up the receiver of his wall phone. The night school secretary is nearly in tears when she realizes who is calling.

"Oh! Oh! You've reconsidered! I can't believe it! Of course, classes have already started, but we can manage something. As soon as I get the word out that you—"

"No. Not that," Harrington says, calmly. "I want to teach English."

She begins to agree with him—"Of course! Of course!"—but stops. "I'm confused. That *is* what you teach. English."

"No. Forgive me. I'm not making myself clear. I want to teach English to the Spanish. Not Literature. Language."

"Oh. Oh. I see. As a second language."

"That's right."

She shuffles some papers, still confused. He means to help, but is still curious himself as to his motivation.

"Now then. All right. This is what you want for now? Or for—"

"For now," he offers, lying. He is very interested in what will be asked next, and what he will answer.

"All right then. Well. Those classes start all the time. No particular schedule. Whenever we get enough students for a class, and find a teacher, we start a new section. You've—ummm—you've taught this before?" She halts herself and chuckles. "Oh, never mind. The book will guide you. It's not like *you* need any help. I haven't been doing this long, but I've never met a teacher who could—"

His cell phone is breaking up, he claims, so he has to get off the line. After he replaces the receiver in the cradle, he goes to take off his suit.

It requires a few weeks to arrange things. For one, he has to study his bookcases. He needs a slight volume, substantial in coverage, but efficient. Nothing but the works themselves will do—no commentaries, no timelines, no essays—only the poetry. He pulls out two that meet the criteria and weighs them in each hand—one red, one chartreuse. The tie is broken by the fact that the chartreuse volume fits most neatly into his coat pocket.

At the same church as before, he teaches the standard amount of time, watching the clock carefully. His students are twenty-three new people, all from the same village in Panama. He is able to make out during the question and answer part of "Adventure 3" that they are relatives of the chair-caners in his previous class. Teaching strictly from the book, he holds up objects and repeats their English equivalents: "watch," "shoe," "shirt"—mostly using items that are on his own person. They learn the names for "cuff link," "wing tip," and "collar stay" before they do "car," "bank" or "house." Their eyes shimmer and they smile big smiles, but thus far they have learned no adjectives of praise. He intends to stay on nouns and pronouns for his entire run.

Dutifully, he closes and locks the door when he leaves the church basement after each class. He walks out behind his students, observing a distance of ten feet. Around the beginning of his third week, he goes through his usual class-ending routine, but when they reach the stairs leading up to the exit, he breaks away and doubles back.

Crossing to the other end of the hall, he climbs the matching staircase that leads to the first floor of the church. At the top, he is met with a janitor, dressed in khaki, his name, Bolivar, in red stitching inside a white oval over his pocket. The man sits slack in his chair, sleeping. One elbow is on the water cooler, resting in a small pool that has not drained away. A cigarette hangs from his lips; his crown rests against a swinging door. At Harrington's cough, one lid peels open. Then, as though its mate has verified the effort, the other peels open too.

"Bolivar," says Harrington.

"Yes?" His voice is fully awake.

Harrington holds up his key. "What kind of key is this?"

The man's head eases forward an inch. He squints, then eases back. "It's just a key."

"Yes. But what will it open? Can I get into the office with it? Or into the church?"

"Is that a key from *here?*" asks the janitor, squinting at it more closely, as though he should have recognized it.

"Yes. It's to my classroom. The one in the basement."

"Oh," says Bolivar. "Then, no. Not to the office. You can only get into the building with it. And your classroom."

"I can get into the building with it?"

"Yes. If you need to. When the church is closed, or not open yet."

Harrington thinks for a moment. "I see. When does that happen?"

Bolivar rolls his eyes backward, to the muffled voices behind the doors.

"I close it after *this* is over."

Harrington listens. "What's that?"

"Some group saying prayers. Then the day man opens it for mass at 7:30."

"Un-hunh. And when are these prayers over?"

Bolivar looks at his watch, drops his wrist, listens. It is quiet.

"Right now," he says. He gets up with difficulty, his knees cracking, and opens the door to poke his head through. Harrington sees it is a back entrance to the sanctuary. The space is already dark, save for a floodlight and a red candle at the altar.

Bolivar lets the door swing shut again and picks up a thermos beside his chair.

"Why," he asks, stopping to look at Harrington, "do you need to stay late?"

Harrington hurries to join him. "Not tonight."

He gives it two more weeks. Every evening, he follows the same routine: teaching, ending, closing, locking, following students out, driving himself home. For some reason, he feels compelled to cough loudly a few times when the students are at their cars, so that they will notice him getting into his own. They waive and say goodbye, pointing him out to the phantom people inside. Harrington waives back, then drives away very slowly, staring into the rearview mirror. He notices that none of the cars turn to the right, as he has; instead, they all turn toward the old apartments and duplexes strung along the highway.

After the two weeks pass, he makes his move. Everything is done in the same pattern, but this time, instead of driving home, he circles the block. He does it so slowly that five minutes pass before he comes around to the entrance again.

The lot is empty; even Bolivar's car is gone; he has made note of which one it is. The front doors to the church are closed fast.

He circles one more time, for good measure and good luck, then shuts the headlights off and whips into the lot, driving along its periphery underneath the bordering trees. He parks the car in an obscure corner, covered with shade.

Using the same key he needs to enter the classroom, he is able to open the aluminum door and slip inside. With a burglar's skill, he tests the door to make sure it is locked again, then leads himself down the hall, hand over hand against one side: to the steps and down, along the expanse of door and wall and door and wall, to the staircase at the opposite end. His feet sound incredibly loud on the stairs—all the louder for the darkness. He rises on tiptoe.

He can tell he is near the landing when he hears the water cooler valve switch on and off. Feeling for it, he puts his finger into the damp, cool porcelain, wetting the tips. Blind, he takes several deep breaths and moves to the swinging door.

It opens silently on the composed flame of the red candle, on the brash beam of the floodlight. The latter bears down on a white-clothed altar and a tabernacle. Hanging above and behind, looming in spectral shadow, is an altar painting. Harrington can make out only its bottom half: bare feet, garment hems, stones. The rest rises into a sheet of smoky dark, hiding the figures, like giant watchers behind a giant veil.

He crosses silently to the fore and stands, waiting for the drumming, coursing of his blood to slacken, to give him room and space to speak. He stares at the curved bronze tabernacle door, where it smolders beneath the streaming light, like coals livened by a dousing of water.

His hand goes into his coat pocket, feeling for the chartreuse volume. Out it comes; he fingers its leaves until he finds the right verse.

"So," he says, looking up, "there you are."

His voice is soft at the beginning, then falls further still.

"And here I am."

He drops one arm to his side. With the other he holds the volume aloft, to the level of his eyes.

At length, his breath pulls and spends, steadily. At last, he cannot feel his heart.

"Now," he says, into the secret silence. "Let's begin."

Cameo

THE FILM WAS CONSIDERED one of the Best of 1973, and consistently cited as a classic of the horror/suspense genre. For her performance, Madeleine was nominated, though she did not win, for all the major acting awards. Afterward, she had made a respectable number of other films, though none as successful, before a six-year run on television in a medical drama. A follow-up sitcom was short-lived—a failure, it was said, due to her lack of comedic flair. There had been a slew of movies-of-the-week, quite portentous for the late eighties, featuring perturbed women, making big choices, about cutting-edge political themes—*Adelaide's Right to Live, The Bag Lady Chronicles*. She had taken an occasional road company tour in *The Glass Menagerie* and *Oklahoma,* and was able to limit her game show appearances to no more than five. Lately, she had championed a line of hand creams on a twenty-four-hour shopping network. That was a move she had been unsure of. But they were paying her a modest sum, and she was won over by how nicely packaged the jars were, wrapped in florist cellophane and tied with blue raffia; that, and the fact that the creams smelled like a chilled fruit plate.

So a respectable career, she had decided; a standard trajectory, well worn by others, but respectable. More B list than A list, but several years on the A list. On top of that, she had managed no more marriages than California culture respected, and had the good taste to keep her current husband for thirty years, which proved she was no tramp. Her plastic surgeries were also of a modest number, and relegated to the skin above her neckline; her breasts and thighs she had girded up herself, rather than have a doctor cut, stitch, or vacuum out. Her children had written no accusatory books, she was being considered for the hostess spot on a charity telethon, and there was rumor of a star on the sidewalk.

"All in all," she would say to herself in bemused comfort, in pensive appraisal. "All in all, a good, long run"—and under the same name she had been born with, Madeleine Moore, thanks to her mother's flawless sense of euphony and alliteration. All that, and one film considered to be a classic. That was enough to walk into judgment with and accept whatever she deserved to get.

Then they had decided to remake it.

"It's been over thirty years," her agent had explained on the phone.

Madeleine shook her head. "I still have clothes in my closet from 1973."

"It's a long time here," said Franklin. "You know that."

She was in the kitchen, padding about in her Isotoner house shoes and an orange beach cover-up that clashed with her pajama pants. She had been making the morning coffee when he called, and was now confused about how many scoops she had counted out. She gave up and dumped the rest of the can into the filter.

"But you don't remake *good* things," she said. "You don't remake what was done right the first time."

Franklin sighed hard. His breath made a cloth-against-microphone sound in her ear.

"That was the old rule, if it ever was the rule."

"Well, it was. Why remake what was well made?"

"What do you mean 'what was done right' and what was 'well made'? *Hamlet*—"

"That's a *play*," Madeleine declared. "A movie only has one life. If it didn't breathe hard the first time, but had promise, *then* you remake it. But not one that reached it's potential. You don't resuscitate a ninety-year-old man. You don't—"

"You're missing the point. These days, they don't remake 'flawed but promising efforts.' They remake what was successful, what has name recognition. If it worked once, it might work again. Because it was successful."

"And where will that leave us? With only one goddamn movie in the end. Just remaking the same goddamn movie, over and over."

"Possibly," said Franklin. "If people keep going to see it, then probably. Anyway, this isn't something I can change."

Madeleine fingered the buttons on the bread machine, a Christmas gift from her son that the maid hadn't learned to use yet.

"Can *I*?"

"What?"

"Can I stop them? Maynard's a lawyer. He *was* a lawyer, anyhow. He still has friends. When he wakes up, I'll—"

"Madeleine. Don't be—unseemly."

"*Unseemly?*" she said, in a voice she at once noted was quite loud enough, was quite shrill enough; no more of that. She straightened her back, swallowed.

"That's what it would be," said Franklin. "Your trying to stop this thing. Getting tangled up with these people, ruining your good name. It would look—it would just look small."

He was a good agent, Franklin was. He'd learned everything from his father, who'd been her agent until he ran his car into the back of a parked tractor. It would indeed look bad, an old woman like her, throwing a fit to keep her crown. It would look petty. In truth, she considered herself very petty and exceedingly small, if the occasion called for it. She would sue them if she could, but there was no way to do it and not look that way.

"Who do they have for my role?" she asked.

The coffee maker gurgled and hissed, choking out black brew, strong as furniture stripper.

"Don't get upset."

"Who?" asked Madeleine, upset. "Not a Chinese girl, or something crazy like that—"

"Don't get—"

"It *is* a Chinese girl!"

"No. It's Morgan's daughter."

Madeleine frowned. Morgan's daughter.

"The swimmer or the tennis player?"

"The swimmer. I think. But she doesn't do that anymore. You know—and you know very well, I might add—that she made an art house movie last year that was well received."

"I know what she did. I *heard* what she did, rather, since I wouldn't *think* of watching it. Of course, if you're willing to do *that*—"

"The script called for it."

"Yes, yes, yes. And it was subtitled in French."

"Don't be so nasty. There's no point in you . . ."

He droned on, but it didn't matter. It was decided. They would remake the one masterwork she had a claim to, and now it would always be a question of "which version did you see?" Side by side at the video store, her classic next to this abomination. And on top of that, with Morgan's daughter in her place, playing her.

"What's the point in telling me this?" she asked.

Franklin waited a moment. "There might be a role for you."

Madeleine lifted her head.

"Well, just a scene, most likely. Something that honors you and the old movie. A nod of respect. But—"

"How disgusting."

"They'd pay you, Madeleine. Maybe we could even get some share—"

"Disgusting. I have more pride—"

"Swallow hard, then," his tone became abrupt, made her blush, "because it *is* going to be a hit, and if you're in it, you'll get some jobs afterward. Grandmothers and kindly neighbors, probably, but work nonetheless. And you need some. You know you do. Plus, Morgan's daughter will have to say all sorts of things in the publicity interviews. 'What an honor it is to work with you' and how you're an 'idol' of hers, and she isn't really *remaking* the role, but only creating her interpretation. Blah-blah-blah. The thing is, people will know you again."

Madeleine said goodbye, that she would call him in a few days.

For a time, she stood at the counter, gulping down mugs of harsh coffee. Then she began washing clean dishes. She plugged the sink, ran hot water into it, made bubbles, and took plates from the cabinet to scrub by hand.

Why take it? She had the telethon possibility. She had the hand creams. And the star in concrete was likely to happen. She was content.

She drew a plate from the sink and began to dry it with a dish towel.

Then again, she'd like the work. The truth was, she needed it, like Franklin said. They hadn't planned well, she and Maynard.

He was old and sleepy and heart-stricken; his blood pressure was way too high. If more money was to come in and save them from downsizing the house, letting the maid go, making up lies about how they didn't have time for the club anymore, she'd have to make it herself.

She stacked the plate on top of the other redundantly clean ones, stared at the column of porcelain. Then she unstopped the sink and let the water siphon down the drain.

She'd like them talking again. She'd like to be interviewed. She'd seen an old rival interviewed not long ago—same age, but with twice as much lifted. The experience was rankling, because as the host fawned about her, some vestal light had fired inside the woman. It shamed Madeleine that she felt this way, and she had not missed it so much until Franklin called, with news that her fullest moment was to be compromised.

She heard Maynard upstairs, groaning as he swung himself up from the mattress. He would sit and stare and scratch for a long time before he attempted to rise. Madeleine dashed the rest of the coffee into the empty sink and made him a small pot of decaf, as the doctor had ordered. She never told Maynard it was decaf.

Above all, if she took the role, she could be the best thing in a bad thing. And maybe it would pique some interest in the old film, if only to make a comparison.

"Don't see the new version," people would say. "It's trash. See the old one."

She opened the cabinet door, lifted the stack of plates and placed them back on the shelf. She brooded until the coffee was nearly ready, then took a mug down for Maynard.

On the other hand, there was something about a remake that went against how she was raised. You weren't supposed to go back—to haunt your own past by trying to relive it—to spoil what was fine by not having the grace to leave it be. And if the film was terrible, wouldn't her appearance somehow diminish the first? She'd be watering down her own wine. And two of anything makes both—

"Coffee?" yelled Maynard. His voice was the only vigorous thing about him anymore.

Madeleine lifted the cup.

"People will know you again," he had said.

★ ★ ★

FOR THE REST OF THE WEEK, Madeleine considered calling the girl. Then she considered calling Morgan instead. There would be talk of them, too, when she made the movie with his child. Maynard had not minded her past. In fact, they had met when he represented her in a tax evasion trial. But he had not known of Morgan, so they ought to get their story straight. Mainly, he ought to get his story straight, so it wouldn't ruin things for her.

She could try to throw the inquisitors off with vague, laughing generalities about "ancient history" and the "prerogatives of youth," but that probably wouldn't work. They weren't easily put off these days. Now they probed and pushed and made up what you wouldn't talk about.

Besides, it wasn't so much questions of her passing romance with Morgan that she was wary about. That had waxed and waned when she was between her second divorce and her marriage to Maynard, between her declining film career and her budding television career; there had been nothing untoward about the relationship. No one had been left or deserted. Even if that *had* been the case, it could only help the movie; these days, indiscretion gilded all it touched. No, the dangerous part was what Morgan had become, and most importantly, had become before they tired of each other.

For one thing, he was very pro-Vietnam. When everyone else was sitting-in and lighting-up, mall-marching and back-turning, Morgan was driving around in a decommissioned army jeep with an American flag brandishing from the back. He took to wearing lapel pins from World War II: "Slap the Jap" and "Bury the Gerry." As if that wasn't enough, he'd had an apple orchard up in the valley, where he worked Mexicans. When the labor movement got wind of it and began to picket his farm, he popped off to the press, calling the protesters "pinkos" and "fleabags"; he said they should spend more time washing their clothes and hair than hanging out around his place. The deal killer was when he started sponsoring, and worse still, participating in a charity rodeo at the state prison. That stirred up both the humane society and the amnesty watch. And each of these blunders took place within one year's time, a firestorm of events that cast him as a warmonger, a slave driver, and a sadist toward two different species, all in short order. After that, his own waning career had been oxidized; he wasn't even fit for "Circus of the Stars" or "Celebrity Password."

If they asked her about her own views at that time, Madeleine wouldn't know what to say. She remembered prickly questions put to her when she was still paired with him. But her mind had been on the new TV offer, and Morgan's entanglements were only a distraction. The story came out that she had distanced herself from his extremist views, but that was not true. They'd spent so little time together—her in town, him up in the valley—that they had naturally parted ways. She didn't even remember having "views" back then, other than ones concerning what was good for her image. She didn't have many now, for that matter, except that she didn't want them tarring her with Morgan's old brush. But it was awkward, since any dissociation from him would look cowardly and tactical. She didn't like that, but shining in Morgan's light would be worse for her present intentions than cowering in the collective shadow of public opinion.

As the date for filming approached, she still had no idea what she would do; she did, however, know what she would wear. She had bought several new outfits, slimming and classic in profile. The stylist had contoured her gray-black hair into a regal bun, and she had bought sleek silver jewelry that set off her sharp features. None of her new stylings would be appropriate for a Victorian-era drama set in a Boston townhouse, but she would at least make a good impression when she arrived and left.

"What is it they want me to play?" Madeleine asked Franklin, the day she was due on the set. He was hard to reach, and she had to use a private number wheedled from his wife.

"Not sure yet. Still in the works."

"What are the ideas, then?"

"Still in formation."

Madeleine narrowed her gaze. "Give me the rough concept. And I don't care how rough."

"Rather than me do that, why don't you give me your thoughts?"

She was standing at the front window, looking for the car they had sent.

"Well, there's that part of the lady who disappears at the train—"

"That's cast," said Franklin.

"Oh. Then the ticket mistress at the—"

"That's cast too."

She grew wary. "What about one of the people who walk through the park during—"

"They've all been cut."

"Cut?"

"Not in the script."

She pressed a hand against the window glass. "They're *changing* things?"

Franklin was quiet, his silence implying he would not go into all that again. Then he said he didn't want to disappoint her, but that she was talking about real roles.

"I didn't say you'd have a *role*. Just an appearance. A cameo. A wink and a nod."

"Yes," said Madeleine. She laid her forehead against the glass too. "Like a joke."

"No. Not like that. Look, I don't have any business speaking for them. Wait and see."

Since they were filming interior shots, the warehouse-sized set was full of booms and scaffolds and trailers of all sorts. At the center was a façade of Back Bay row houses, and to the side, box sets of a Victorian entry, parlor, and bedroom. The whole place was dark and wintry-looking, and the flood lamps pitched a fierce, cutting light over the lot. When they had made the original, they filmed the entire thing in Boston; so this was something else they had changed.

Still, they were kind to Madeleine when she arrived; a nice flourish of concern and esteem. The director came over, a slender young man with a foreign name, and the lead actor came out, a large older man in a foreign suit. They set her in a chair, brought her some cappuccino, and told her she could watch, if she liked, but there was a trailer for her use if she didn't. A trailer all her own. Franklin was a good agent.

She opened the door and climbed inside, looked in the refrigerator and sat on the bed, called to check if Maynard had taken his noon medicine, then returned to watch the shoot.

The scenes mostly involved the specter, which was the menace in the film. In her day, they had simply implied its presence by the reaction of the players; but now they were using a computer-generated ghost, which required some sort of blue screen and endless shots of the set. On the whole, it was very boring, and there was no sign of the girl all day. She might have been inside her trailer, for all Madeleine knew, and she cast an eye toward it every so often.

Toward six, the director, Stefan, came over and said she could go home. Perhaps they would use her tomorrow. When she asked in what way, he suggested a patrician lady, leaving the house as the heroine entered it—a brief but pregnant exchange between the two actresses who had undertaken this historic role. Madeleine slept well on the news, since she would get to speak.

But two more days passed, and when she asked again, Stefan said that she might play a visiting aunt instead, one of the guests the heroine greets at a ball.

"Any lines?" she asked.

"A few words. Maybe. But mostly a long, lingering stare."

He added that she might reappear in the film later, for another lingering stare.

The news dispirited Madeleine, but she resolved to wait it out. He might go back to his original idea, or come up with something more substantial; the boy's mind changed so much that it was likely. One minute he would shoot from one angle, the next from the opposite, and the next from the first angle again, but with the actors in different places. They had money to burn, she realized, another change from her day, or at least a change from the kind of pictures she'd been cast in. In truth, it was not the same movie at all. They were changing so much, she could recognize only the same basic form, but not the same character.

Every morning the car arrived and every morning Madeleine met it, having risen hours before to dress herself and to fix Maynard. His feet and calves swelled if he didn't put constriction hose on, and he couldn't stoop down far enough to get them over his toes. She also had to fix his low-sodium lunch and snacks in individual baggies, with a picture of a clock taped to each so that the Salvadoran maid could tell what time to give them to him. Finally, she had to measure out the heap of pills he took throughout the day, carefully dropping them into a segmented box, labeled by meals. Despite her precautions, she didn't trust the maid or Maynard either, and called every few hours to confirm he'd taken what he was supposed to.

A week passed, with no more news of her appearance and no more conjecture from Stefan. He would hurry by, quickly but politely, calling out as he skipped backward: "Any day now. Any day."

"Leave the boy alone, Madeleine," Franklin said, when she called to complain of her disuse. "Play it cool. You're there, and he's promised, and the longer you're cool, the more he'll owe you. Has the girl shown up yet?"

Madeleine said no, and that was another thing.

"What kind of schedule is this, with the star never here, and the extras and the computer doing all the work?"

Times were different, she was informed, and the girl would appear soon. Madeleine was to call Franklin when she did in fact arrive. He had an idea.

"What kind of idea? And how do you know *soon?* She hasn't so much as set—"

But he said he just knew and begged off the line.

He was as good as his prophecy, though, as the girl materialized that very afternoon. She stood talking to a script girl close to the townhouse façade. Madeleine stepped behind the trailer to peek without being seen.

She was buxom enough, but pale, drawn-looking, bland, apathetic, and peculiarly aged, like someone who had been too hard on her body. In fact, from what Madeleine understood, she had let others, many, be too hard on her body, in all sorts of ways. For a girl so young, she moved like an old lady, careful of herself as she walked on ice or edged over broken ground. It was as though she carried in her body the memory of a hard fall, which made her tentative and chary. Still and all, she was Morgan's daughter. The cut of her face—aquiline nose, squared-off chin, high forehead—Madeleine had known his face well, and knew it again in this girl's. Her best feature was her thick chestnut hair, but it was cut all raggedy, and she could have used a brush.

Madeleine picked her way through the snakes of cable behind the trailer and made her entrance from the other side, so the girl would see her. Summoning her old poise-school training—chin high, shoulders back—she took one of the chairs just outside the filming perimeter and pretended to thumb through the script. The girl haunted her peripheral vision for a time, then loomed closer.

"Miss Moore?"

"Yes?" said Madeleine, looking up. She let her eyes brighten when they locked gazes.

"Oh. Yes, yes."

"I'm—"

"Yes, of course you are," said Madeleine, and began to stand. But the girl sent a shaky hand out for the chair beside her and crept into the seat. She took a minute to situate herself, the way Maynard would do whenever he sat.

"I've been looking forward to meeting you," said Madeleine.

The girl nodded. Her face was still unsettled, as though one of her joints hadn't stabilized.

"They haven't needed me, so I've been . . ." she shook her head. "God I'm sore."

Madeleine nodded, unsure of what to say.

"Well, you're so active, I guess that's—"

"What?"

"You swim so much, I mean," offered Madeleine. "You used to swim, at least."

The girl made an ugly frown. "What?"

"Wasn't that—wasn't that you who went to the Olympics?"

The girl shook her head, began to knead the muscles in her thighs. "That was my sister."

"Oh," said Madeleine. "I was misled, then. You're the tennis player."

The girl cocked her head a bit.

"How do you know so much?"

"You were both in the paper a lot. You were—"

"A long time ago," she said, massaging the other thigh. "I was just out all night."

The girl sat up all of a sudden, her face tight. She drilled her gaze into Madeleine.

"Do you stay in touch with Daddy?"

"I beg your pardon?"

"You knew him well."

Gauche, Madeleine thought. She looked away, took up the script again.

"We all knew each other then. It was a smaller place. And *no,* I don't stay in touch."

"It was more than that," said the girl. "I didn't know about it until they told me."

"Who told you?" asked Madeleine, her own face tight now, and her tone as blunt as the girl's. "And told you what?"

"Franklin. He's my agent too."

Madeleine nodded. She would beat him up one side and down the other when she got away from here. He had arranged this whole business.

"He said you were together for a time, back then. Is 'engaged' too big a word for it?"

"It is," said Madeleine, and excused herself to go inside the trailer. She had to check on Maynard; she had to call Franklin; she had to cool the blush out of her face.

It took twenty whole minutes, Franklin being unreachable and Maynard being unperturbed, but when she came back out, the girl was still there. An entourage of minions, two with cameras, swarmed about her; one had brushed her hair, somewhat, and had fixed her face. She sat in the same seat, in the same position, but holding a diet drink can between her hands, like a chalice. She stared dead at Madeleine; there was nowhere else to go but to the seat again—head up, shoulders back.

"He's living in Colorado these days," said the girl. The picture takers snapped several shots; Madeleine gave them her profile.

"Is that right?"

"With his new wife."

"Oh? I didn't know your mother and he—"

"No. She died."

The girl took a long, slow sip, feeling the ridge of the can with her top lip, as if the cold drink were piping hot.

"Oh. I'm sorry," said Madeleine.

"It's been several years now. Did you know Mama?"

"No, she was long after," she checked herself. "She wasn't in show business, of course. Do you see him much yourself?"

"Not lately." She sat back. "He's not pleased with me."

What's there to be pleased with, Madeleine thought. Despite the makeup, there was rheum in the girl's eyes, and she was wearing clothes she looked to have slept in.

"He didn't want me to get into all this," she said, and glanced out at the set, nodding her head at it. She looked back at Madeleine. "I didn't have to, you know. I went to college."

Madeleine smiled.

"I didn't graduate, but I did go. I had good grades. My first year."

"Of course."

"Then I got some bad habits my second year and couldn't shake them." She looked back at the set, nodded again, in scorn. "That's what led me to this."

Madeleine bridled a bit, insulted in a backward way.

"You know what I wanted to do?" the girl asked and sat up straight.

"No."

"You won't believe it."

Madeleine smiled with half of her mouth, shrugged.

"I wanted to be an accountant. I used to be very good at putting things in order. I like keeping books and—"

"You do that still?"

"What?"

"Keep books. You said—"

"Oh. Oh no. I—they do that for me." She looked off and took another languid sip. "I wouldn't trust myself now."

The conversation was growing odd and slightly morose, so Madeleine was thankful when Stefan called her over. With him was the lead actor, dressed in period tails, boots, and cravat.

"I know how to make a big statement," said Stefan, grinning. "How to have a deep impact. Harry here is an artist—in the film, that is—right? So what if he's painting your picture? What if you're a lady who's in the house from time to time, sitting for your portrait?"

Madeleine sighed at another change for the worse. She wanted to ask about lines; even the slightest would flesh her out some, whomever she played. But at least the boy seemed adamant, and if she could just get into the film, finally, in whatever way, it would be better than this aimless hovering about. She would at least earn her check.

"So," she said, "when do we get started?"

"Tomorrow. Maybe. We need to figure wardrobe. Hang around and we'll send for you."

Madeleine nodded, turned, picked her way back through snack carts and around booms.

If she complained of this constant lessening, Franklin would only remind her that she was getting paid either way—mouth shut or mouth open. Besides, the point was to revive her in the public view. Furthermore, she was tired of complaining, tired of hearing herself take the part of a fading—no, faded—old woman whose histrionics revealed she had no idea as to where she really stood in the world. She was tired of being so typical.

When she came around the side of her trailer, the girl and a new suite of attendants were barring her way. And she was in full costume now, from boostier to bustle, an outfit Madeleine remembered well. The wardrobe master was assessing the fit as a seamstress pinched and gathered cloth at her waist.

"He thinks I'm a prostitute," the girl said, wobbling as the seamstress snatched at the bustle.

"Who does?" asked Madeleine, sighing. She just up and said this kind of thing?

"Daddy."

Madeleine stepped around a rack of clothes. "Well. That's a bit extreme."

The girl tottered about, so as to face Madeleine; the seamstress shuffled in tow.

"But only a bit," she laughed. "Did you see my last movie?"

Madeleine thought the girl took too much pleasure in saying that and was once again disgusted. If she could just get in the trailer. She grabbed another rack they had wheeled in front of the door and yanked it aside.

"Most things get patched up over time," said Madeleine, pushing past the rack and the now kneeling seamstress.

"If you think about it, he's right," said the girl.

"Wait until Christmas." Madeleine opened the door. "People always reconcile around—"

"I take money for things men like to see. That's really why they wanted me for this film."

"Christmas will solve everything."

Madeleine climbed in and shut the door. She felt like spitting. Foul little slut. It was like watching a pig wallow around in your wedding dress. She wanted to say so, and did say so to Maynard that night.

He sat in his easy chair, next to the bed, as she stripped the constriction hose off his legs.

"And she stands there, wearing what I wore—the very same dress, right down to that shade of plum—and playing my role, while I wander around like a fool, and—"

Maynard winced. "Don't pull so hard, dammit."

She apologized and massaged his legs to rub out the ribs that had runneled his flesh. His skin was a strange, old ivory now. When she touched it, it went a bluish white.

"And then she has the nerve to tell me that she's going to 'sex it up,' which we know she is fully qualified to do. I have half a mind to quit the whole thing."

"Rub deeper," said Maynard. He lay back in the chair. "What difference is it to you, what she says?"

Madeleine glared at him; she would not rub deeper. "You and Franklin. You might as well *be* Franklin, the way you talk. The one thing that showed what I was capable of, the one thing that showed what I could've done—"

Maynard shook his head. "That you could pretend better than you had a reputation for pretending. Big deal."

"I knew you'd say that," said Madeleine; Maynard hated actors. She switched to his other leg and began to work the flesh there.

"I didn't get to do much, God knows. But there was one thing that showed who I was, and—"

"I'll tell you who you are," said Maynard.

She stopped her kneading, looked up. His face was sheepish.

"You're the only one who can get me some more pills."

"What?"

He looked away. "I spilled them down the sink."

"What?"

"The blue ones. I spilled them down the sink."

She lowered his foot to the floor, stared at him until he looked her in the face again.

A few months ago, she would have been exasperated when this kind of thing happened, which it did more and more. His pills—especially the tiny blue ones—were expensive, the insurance card didn't cover them, and the hand cream money didn't make up the difference. But since his fingers weren't working well, or his eyes either, and since the best light was in the bathroom, right over the sink—where she told him time and again not to open his pills, for this very reason—still, there was no point saying it.

She stood up, waited by as Maynard hoisted himself to his feet.

So she would have yet another fight with a doctor or a pharmacist, a repeat performance about the same old thing. She had fought with a legion of them over the past few years, and chewed out all kinds of insurance adjusters. But not once had she failed to get the prescriptions refilled; not once had Maynard failed to see the doctor when he needed to, with no waiting. And best of all, not once had she resorted to using her name or face to get what she wanted. She hadn't needed to.

He crawled into bed, turned the covers down on her side.

She would have to do it again.

★ ★ ★

Madeleine WAITED OUTSIDE HER TRAILER, watching men dump trash bags full of plastic snow onto the walk in front of the townhouses. Others had climbed onto the roof and were emptying bags along the eaves, shimmering flakes against the window ledges. The stage crew had muffled all of the floodlights, lessened all of the gas lamps at the street corners. The scene was dimmer, colder than mid-winter; it was mid-winter in eclipse, as though the sun had turned sideways to the world, indifferent to its dependency.

It was close to noon, and the girl had not yet appeared. The set was devoted to more footage of the specter, so only the interior sets were in use—transition shots mostly, of maids emptying chamber pots, of guests sipping tea, and if they got to it, of a lady's portrait being painted. To that end, Stefan had costumed Madeleine in mourning clothes: yards of black taffeta, a black lace mantilla, and an antique mourning broach made of braided black hair. With her own hair clasped at the nape of her neck, Madeleine looked twice her age and felt three times it.

The bustle made it hard to sit in the armchairs, so they had to bring a workman's stool over for her to perch on. It also made it hard to stand and escape when the girl finally emerged from the darkened corners of the set. She was wearing the same clothes as the day before, or something so similar it might well have been: jeans, boots, a shrunken T-shirt that exposed her waist, and bangles on her wrists. She made straight for Madeleine, creeping along in her broken, decrepit gait.

"House party," she said, drawing closer. Her voice was scratchy. She cleared it as she stopped and listed against the trailer wall.

Madeleine pretended to watch the men work for a good five-second count, then lazily turned toward the girl.

"You're trying to tell me you've been to a house party?" she asked, cool.

The girl nodded.

"Whose house?"

She cocked her head, shrugged, like she was as surprised to be asked as she was not to know. Madeleine turned away again, faintly pleased with herself.

Some actors were in the parlor, finding their marks and walking through their lines. One was the scheming neighbor and the other was the son of the cook, the two characters next to die in the script. According to the pattern, the specter had already done in the scullery maid and the ticket-mistress. Today they were lounging around in street clothes, cozying up to Stefan.

Madeleine glanced at her watch, hidden beneath her sleeve ruff.

If he didn't start shooting the footage of her portrait, it would be lunchtime. And if it got to be lunchtime before she called the doctor's office, they would not call her back. She had only been able to salvage a day's worth of spilt pills from the bathroom floor and wastebasket.

"You ended on good terms, didn't you? You and Daddy?"

Madeleine's gaze shot up. She stared hard at the girl, in hopes of shaming her.

"Of course we did. Of course. But I really don't want—"

"So he would—if you were to see him—he would talk to you?"

Madeleine frowned, shook her head. "Of *course* he would. Why would you ask that?"

The girl broke into a smile; her eyes brightened. She lurched from the trailer wall and slunk down beside Madeleine in a squat, wincing as she took the posture.

"You know," she began. "I was surprised when I heard you were going to be in this."

Madeleine wanted to draw away, but the dress and stool held her.

"Why?"

"I was just surprised you'd take this walk-on. That's all."

"Well, I did it out of—homage—in a way."

The girl smiled, winked, as if she knew better. Madeleine was repulsed.

"But then Franklin said you knew that *I* was considering it—and since you and Daddy—well, you know. So when I heard *that*—and I knew that's why *you* were—because of *me*. Well, then that's why I decided to do it too."

"Yes. Well," said Madeleine, unsure, "of course, it was nice of them to want to honor the old film, too. By having me in it. And—"

The girl's face changed. She drew even closer, her eyes shifty, conspiratorial. Madeleine couldn't believe the presumption.

"Since we're friends," she said, softly, "I want you to know something."

Friends? thought Madeleine.

"Stefan wants to seem that way—*honor-bound*. He wants it to look like that. But it's just the slightest, most insincere act he could muster."

Madeleine's stomach turned. She looked off, spotted Stefan in his director's chair. He was getting a back rub from the scullery maid as he munched on a panini.

"It's not just you, though," the girl continued. "He keeps saying the script calls for me to show my tits. That it's warranted. But I know for a fact he rewrote that whole first scene to put in some kind of *mother's milk* symbol, just so he could persuade me there was a reason."

"What?"

The girl nodded, fierce. "That wasn't in the first version, was it? Your version?"

"What wasn't?"

"That calf they brought in the other day? See? It's my tits. I think he—"

"Don't tell me about that," said Madeleine, struggling up from the stool.

"It's the truth. He won't admit it, but it's a ploy." The girl looked down at her chest.

"I've got nice tits."

"Excuse me," said Madeleine, gathering her skirts away from the girl. "I have to go to the . . . I have to make a phone call."

She slammed the trailer door, grabbed her purse from the

banquette and dug around for her phone. She hadn't been able to get Franklin for a week, but she would hold on the line all day if she had to. She would hold on the line like a bill collector on the last day of the month until he took the call.

But just as she pressed in the final number, she stopped and hung up again. It was noon. She had to call the doctor's office.

Once again she rummaged through her purse, but this time, to find the doctor's card. She nearly ripped it in half as she pulled it from her wallet.

Just let them try it, she thought, seething. Just let them try to brush her off. She was too good at this. She was on old hand at this role; she'd played it too many times. And when they answered, she was in luck; the doctor was available. At first he attempted to object, questioning her motives, but Madeleine was in no mood.

"Just exactly what are you implying?" she snapped, then listened. "Well, he most certainly is *not* addicted to these things. Who would want to be? God knows, there are better ways to get high or fall asleep than Progesterine."

The doctor then took a cool, inquisitorial tone, which made her all the more furious.

"What? He *spilt* them. What? Down the sink. Do you want to come take the drain apart to see? I'll tell you what. I want you to come over—in fact, I'll come get you. Where do you live? I have a pencil. Tell me. No, I want you to. I *insist* you come over to my house and open the drain. What? Why, I think it *is* necessary, to satisfy yourself that my husband, a seventy-five year old heart patient, a respected—well-respected—member of the bar, and a taxpayer to satisfy yourself he isn't a drug addict. No. I *insist*."

In the end, the doctor said he would call in the prescription, though the pharmacist couldn't fill it until the next day.

Madeleine hung up the phone, triumphant and lustrous in her victory. She stripped off the widow's weeds, arrayed herself in her new clothes and jewelry, and left the set, saying only that she had something planned with her husband. Her glow carried on into the night.

Maynard sat at the dinner table, before a plate of saltless fish and stewed tomatoes. He smiled as Madeleine related her conversation with the doctor. She also gave him his instructions for tomorrow, and in the mildly imperious tone she took whenever she had things in hand: a general in conquest who, despite the celebrations, had begun marshaling practicalities, setting out priorities in a craggy good humor.

"Now, I can't pick the pills up tomorrow, Maynard. You'll have to do it yourself. But if they give you any trouble at all, any at all, you call me. I have to be on the set, but things should be just as I've explained them. And the minute you get the prescription, the very minute, you call me. You'll be late taking the dosage as it is."

"Okay," he said, pushing his fish around. She noticed and told him to eat it. He did.

Madeleine mulled for a moment. The last time Maynard had gone by himself to pick up his Progesterine, he let them give him Phrygesterine, a milk enhancer for nursing mothers.

"In fact," she said, reconsidering. "I want you to come to the set. I want you to show me that you got the right ones."

"What?" said Maynard. "Why the hell—"

"I'll get a pass for you tomorrow. You come by the set and show me."

"I don't want to come by the—"

"Yes. I'll worry all day if you don't. If you just call, I'll worry if you got the right thing. You better come by the set to show me."

"Goddamanit," said Maynard. "I'm not an idiot. I made one mistake. Okay, two, but—"

"I insist. You won't read the dosage either. It might've changed. You'll go and overdose yourself and then I'll *really* have something to explain the next time."

They fought all the way to bed, but Maynard gave over when she offered to let him take a nap in the trailer and watch baseball on the plasma TV.

The next day, Madeleine was back in costume, ready for her portrait scene. It was scheduled for the morning, but things dragged on while Stefan and the computer men worked with the ghost and the blue screen.

In the meantime, it was a press day. A reporter from one of the entertainment programs was filming interviews in a corner of the set. Madeleine was surprised to hear he wanted to talk to her too, not just the leads. So she waited around nearby, watching the spiky-haired man question Harry; the two of them sat on facing stools.

"Are they done yet?"

Madeleine jumped. The girl had sneaked up to stand at her elbow. She was in the plum costume again, her hair teased and piled high. Her breasts had been forced up to the top of her bodice. Madeleine turned away.

"They just got started."

"Good," she said, then put her hands on her waist and pulled hard breaths, to get air into her corseted lungs. Madeleine looked askance. The girl seemed as pained standing still as she normally did when moving.

"Those things are tight, aren't they?"

The girl nodded, smiled with difficulty.

"Don't breathe so deep," offered Madeleine. "Pushing against it won't help, and you'll get panicky after a while. Take shallow breaths until you find a pattern."

The girl slowed her pace until it was manageable. She thanked Madeleine, and they watched the interview for a time, side by side. At length, she edged closer.

"Did I upset you yesterday?" she asked, her voice low.

Madeleine shook her head.

"Yes, I did."

"No, you didn't."

The girl nodded, then after a moment asked again.

"Are you mad at Franklin, then?"

Madeleine shrugged one shoulder.

"Don't be. He said I should meet you."

"Did he now?"

"He said this would be a good springboard for me."

Madeleine snorted. "He meant *I* would be a good springboard for you. Remaking my film. Remaking my role. He thinks people like to watch history repeat itself."

The girl looked down. "Well, I didn't mean it that way. I didn't even know about you until he told me."

"Thank you," said Madeleine.

"That didn't come out right. I knew who you *were*. I just didn't know about this film. And I didn't care about remaking it. Not at all. But then he told me about you and Daddy."

Madeleine blushed.

"He's got a bee farm out there. In Colorado. He . . ."

The girl winced. She was talking too much, trying to speak too fast; the corset got the best of her. She was as pale as Maynard now. Madeleine motioned her to sit atop a nearby tool chest and then took a seat beside her.

"He's still farming then," said Madeleine, while the girl was collecting herself. "He had that orchard up in the valley. Breathe shallow, through your nose."

The girl pulled and blew. "Well," she said, "he's from Texas."

"Yes. He was always very proud of that."

"And he never liked it here."

"No. I don't think he ever did."

"He didn't think acting was very manly."

Madeleine smiled. "It's a shame he was so successful at something he didn't want to do."

The girl nodded. "He should never have left Texas."

A loud noise rang out as the lunch wagon opened its doors. Madeleine looked at her watch. The day was slipping past, faster than she expected. All of the days on this set slipped by fast, just the opposite of the way it used to seem. They used to film and film and film, and stay late into the night and rise early in the day. She heard they still did that, had thought it would be so here, but it had not. Everything went fast here. Madeleine was tired all of a sudden and winded herself. She propped her elbow on her knee and rested her chin in her hand.

"I think he got talked into leaving it," she said. "He was a handsome man, and in those days, that was enough for people to insist you leave for a bigger town."

The girl struggled upright, her hands on her waist. "Who? Who would insist?"

Madeleine flinched. This girl made her nervous. She was too anxious, too impatient for replies. Say the most casual thing, the most innocent of observations, and she bristled up as though you meant to convey a clue or a message, as if someone had told her she should be listening for things. As if happiness lay in hearing some right thing said. Madeleine shrugged, thought of what she had meant.

"Well, everybody would. In small places, that is. You'd get a reputation. They'd hand you your destiny like a train ticket—'You won't be here long. You're looking for a bigger town.' It was sweet really; humble of them; like anything glorious was out of place if it wasn't in a real city, under lots of lights. They meant well."

The girl sat back, nodding, staring. "That's what happened to him, then."

"I . . well, it's just my opinion. Just an observation. It's not my place to say."

"Is that what happened to you, too? That's your place to say."

Madeleine blinked. "I didn't need to be talked into anything. I was always willing."

The interviewer was done with Harry. He beckoned to the girl, who mustered the strength to rise, steadying herself on Madeleine's shoulder. Madeleine rose too and walked with her a ways, to keep her stable.

She stayed close to listen to the interviewer's questions: What did this project mean to her career? What did she think of Stefan? What was it like to be in a period costume drama? Did she believe in ghosts herself?

The only interesting question was what, as Morgan's daughter, she thought about working with Madeleine Moore and assuming her old role. The girl was gracious, saying just what Franklin had said she would: Madeleine was an idol—it was an honor—no one could remake her classic performance, but only reinterpret the part. When she finished, she climbed off the stool and came back to Madeleine. She was already pulling the pins out of her hair.

"They made me get dressed up just for this," she said, as her chestnut hair fell. She looked more sanguine now, had better color. "After I get this off, I'm leaving."

When Madeleine asked where she was going, the girl said back to the house party. It had lasted for three days and was still going.

"Didn't you do that yesterday?"

"Yes."

"You want to do it again?"

She paused, cocked her head. "I do it every day."

"The same thing? Every day?"

"Yes."

"You'll wear yourself out."

The girl supposed that she would, but then everybody did. She ventured that in another time, Madeleine would have come along too. It was good for your career.

Madeleine sighed.

"That's a very true cliché," said the girl.

"Most are," nodded Madeleine. "They're easy to recognize. They're easy to be, for that matter. I was never able to make an exception of myself."

"Everybody crowded into the same composite, then," the girl said, smiling. "To be noticed for the same things."

"That's right. Otherwise, you're an aberration—a bump on the nose. You'd spoil the picture."

The girl looked winsome now.

"That's what ended Daddy. But it's just as well."

"Yes. It's a very parochial place."

The girl laughed again. "What rebels we all are."

"Yes, very brave."

"To tell you the truth, I'd rather keep bees."

"Than be one?"

"Yes, Yes."

"Well," said Madeleine. "Well."

"But I'm not brave enough either," said the girl, and she gathered her skirts and slipped away into the darkened set.

It was Madeleine's turn now. She took the stool in front of the interviewer, ready for him to begin. Instead, he just sat there, smiling and drumming his fingers on his note cards.

"I'm all set," she hinted.

"Just have to wait for a few things," he answered.

But the cameraman was in place, and the crew was on standby; Madeleine couldn't imagine why they were waiting.

"In the meantime," said the man, "here are some of the questions I'll ask."

He handed her a card. Madeleine squinted to read it, as she didn't have her glasses on:

    —*What does this project mean to your career?*

    —*What do you think of working with Stefan Van Stander?*

    —*What's it like to be in a period costume drama?*

    —*Do you believe in ghosts?*

She glanced up at the interviewer, who preserved a vapid smile.

"But these are the same things you asked her."

He nodded. "Harry, too. There's only so much to ask, at this point."

Madeleine handed the card back.

"There's nothing to distinguish one from the other, then."

He bunched his mouth. "Well, that's not completely true," he said, and leaned over to show Madeleine another card.

"See? It's the same outline, but there's a space here for a question that's exclusive to whoever sits in that place." He drew back, satisfied. "That's the spirit of the interview."

Madeleine nodded. He stared at her, smiling.

"What are we waiting for then?" she asked.

"For your spirit to drop into that space."

In time, an assistant brought him a note. And from the questions that she was eventually asked, she could tell Franklin had written them. They sounded like him.

What's it like working with Morgan's daughter? What was between Morgan and you, back then? How does it feel to watch her in your old role?

Madeleine was as gracious as the girl had been, and was ready to climb off the stool and be done with it when he stopped her with one last question.

"Did you know he's dropping by the set today? It's a surprise. For the both of you." Madeleine stared. She shook her head, then looked about for the girl, who had disappeared.

"You better tell her. She's on her way to—"

"Oh, we will. Somebody's finding her now. We want a reunion shot. The three of you."

After that, the afternoon galloped past. What on any other day would have been hours of pointless waiting around in costume was filled with flurry, and all of it about her: Madeleine was taken back to the makeup chair, back to the hairdresser, back to the seamstress. She was made more pallid, more severe, more altogether widowish. And when they were done, they led her over to the parlor set, where Stefan and Harry were waiting. The men stood before a large, white, silk screen, which was blocking the fireplace. Harry held a stylus and an ink bottle.

"What's this?" asked Madeleine, looking around for an easel and canvas.

Stefan smiled. "I've changed my mind. Instead of a portraitist, Harry's a silhouette maker. It's more meaningful."

He took Madeleine by the hand, led her behind the screen

and sat her on a needlepoint bench. A fierce spotlight crouched on the floor at her feet.

"Now," said Stefan. "Turn sideways. We want your profile."

Madeleine was wide-eyed, bewildered.

"But you can't see me," she said. "Nobody will recognize me."

Stefan shook his head. "People who know you will."

"But they *already* know me."

He took her chin and posed her head up, took her shoulders and rolled them back.

"That's right. You're a star. Okay, let's roll."

Madeleine held stock still, the light scorching the right side of her body. She could see nothing, as everyone else was on the other side of the screen. She could only hear the interviewer, asking the same questions to another member of the cast. And why not? Though they were filming, there was no need for quiet. There were no lines, nothing to say.

"What's it like to be in a period costume drama?" he asked. "Do you believe in ghosts?"

The heat from the footlight made Madeleine loose at the joints, flattened and pressed.

She had said she never believed in ghosts and left the silly question at that. But now she thought the ghost had a bigger role than she. And for a sorry moment she was jealous of it, even sympathetic with its feeble mimicry, with the reaction it caused in those frightened by its notice.

She began to sweat, melt, evaporate. At length, she heard someone enter the set, some guest being greeted.

Morgan, she decided, and burned with shame over what she had let be said, and over her sitting there, an old shadow inside an old shadow, with nothing new to see, nothing at all to say.

Then she heard her name called, herself recognized, and she listened as deficient steps approached her from the other side of the screen.

"Hey. Hey," came Maynard's voice, rattling his paper bag. "I got it. See?"

A Thing of Beauty

*F*IRST, *YOU'RE FIRED. You're not only fired, but also have lost all benefits, existing and accumulated. These losses are retroactive. You are covered for nothing—home, health, auto, death. There will be no references, and letters have been sent to potential employers, informing them of your gross ineptitude. The IRS was notified of irregularities, and the federal prosecutor is looking into your case. Your children have been taken, your husband has left, and your house has been foreclosed on. Your car is seized, your assets, frozen. You have a dread disease, and without a place to be buried (remember that insurance part?), your corpse will be thrown into a remote ditch. Finally, your soul is bound for hell, last ring, next to Brutus. That's pretty much it. For now. And don't play innocent. You know why this is happening. You know what this is for.*

It was not a dream, this threat. Helena never had it when she was asleep. Her nightmares were of a more ordinary stripe: being knocked off a cliff by a shaggy white goat, being stalked through a department store by a bald dwarf with bloody fangs. Instead, this threat belonged to the day—a sourceless but certain retaliation yet to be visited upon her. It had even filled itself in over the years with dreadful particularity; just recently had it included her damnation. And though its torment was in the nature of a sensitive tooth—always present, though not always immediate—it could become most acute whenever she felt on the verge of being discovered, of being exposed by the shadowy powers that ran the universe. No crime was worse, in her view, than the one she committed every day, simply by being.

In truth, some of her fears were past realization. Her children were grown and gone. At sixty-five, her retired, ESPN-bound husband would not leave her. And the house was paid for. They'd had a mortgage-burning party, with diet Shasta and a box of petits fours as refreshments. Their retirement was in government securities—assured of low return, but assured nonetheless.

Still, it was several years yet before she could quit her job as a financial advisor at the bank, a job she had no idea how to do.

During the brief, relatively carefree time of her life, before the threat became so large and particular, Helena had been a teller at a bank in downtown Memphis. An adding machine was all she really needed back then—that, and a stool with a padded back. But during a financial crisis in the seventies, a bus had killed three of the bank's financial advisors on their way back from lunch at a nearby chicken shack. Instead of hiring new ones, the bank had promoted Helena. And since then, it had taken an everlasting parade of tricks to throw folks off her trail. For years they had worked, but she was less and less sure of herself. And if they found out now, she and Baxter would not be able to manage. If he lost cable, they would be forced to have more regular conversations, which was an excruciating business. And it was a real possibility, now that she could not hear very well.

No matter what the doctor said, she knew people could notice her hearing aids. After all, the things whistled and buzzed like an oven timer. Although she had always worn her gray hair in a bun, gathered at her crown, she'd had to pull it down into a page-boy, to cover her ears, and hence her hearing aids. But the style didn't suit her. Her face was too jowly, and her eyes too dreary brown and wide-set for a look so young. Accustomed to conservative sweaters, blouses, and skirts, she'd tried to adopt a younger style of clothes, to match her hair: cowl necks or mock turtles, big belts with bigger buckles, scarves in animal prints and boots and slacks that zipped up at the side. She was too pear-shaped for all of these, she knew, but wore them to match the absurd hairstyle. All had been sacrificed to this scheme, this necessary farce, because she could not seem so old that she could not hear. They might then become suspicious, start to explain her mistakes in terms of her age. And that might warrant an even closer look, at both what she was doing and what she had done. How far back would they go? It couldn't be risked. They might find out, and there was too much to find out.

For one thing, she could not add—except on her fingers. Despite her father's tireless efforts with flash cards, she had never memorized the tables. She would put her hands behind her back, and with a deft skill that required she only fidget her fingertips, scale up to ten, doubling as necessary. Subtraction required feeling her fingers fold toward her palm, one by one, like a line of felled trees. Now, when asked to calculate something away from her desk, it took elaborate tricks to get back to her adding machine. She rounded up a great deal.

For another thing, she didn't really know how to read financial statements or how to amortize. Depreciation was a mystery, no matter how many times she tried to teach herself (*You mean a perfectly good car is worth nothing?* she would privately object). And when asked to recommend mutual funds, she would send out a set of explanatory graphs rather than explain. These she collected from web sites in massive numbers. The thicker the envelope, the more secure she felt in having inundated her potential unmasker.

Her fraudulence didn't stop at work, either. At home, she was worse. She couldn't even account for her twin daughters' birthday. Her husband had been away in the army when the time came, and she had moved to his base right after their birth. But time passed. The babies had to go to the doctor, and for her life she couldn't remember the day to put on the records. So she had made one up, then forgotten it. On another occasion, she was required to do the same, so she had to guess at the first. In time, she'd written down an invented date and taped it to the inside of the closet door. She knew she could send off for the birth certificate, but by then there had been several birthdays. She felt terrible whenever sweet sixteen or voting age or some other milestone rolled around. It could all be untrue.

But these faults in her nature, and many others, she could have lived with. Some gauntlets were harder to run than others, but she had managed all the way to this near-end of her life. The problem was that on top everything else, there was something worse. The fact was, she could go in and out. Not just her hearing. Her. She could disappear.

The phenomenon was not in her imagination, and she was not insane, though she thought at times it would drive her so. She was not epileptic, either. She'd had that checked when still a girl. Her mother was the only one she'd ever confessed the malady to, and then only after ten years of having first noticed it.

Stricken white by the news, the woman had sat down hard on a kitchen chair. Helena fidgeted in remorse, wanting to take it back. Even when they'd returned from the doctor with news he'd expected would cheer them: "She's fine, nothing extraordinary, just a girls' lightheadedness, I imagine." Neither could bear to talk of it. The disappointment that it was not medically explainable had been nerve-shattering. It had driven her mother into a frenzy that she took out on the lawn. She mowed it daily until it reached a golf green's height, then set to barbering the hedges with a severity that implied she'd found their very existence insulting. Helena had watched her from the window—at her stooped frame dodging in and about the bushes, madly, her wild gray hair flying about like a lunatic's. Helena had rushed outside, unable to bear any more of it.

"You mean you find these *fits* pleasurable?" her mother had asked, gasping for air. The hedge sheers, she'd clinched hard in a palsied grip.

Helena bowed her head.

"Do you know what I mean by *pleasurable?*" her mother asked.

She was only fifteen, and in those days she was expected not to know. In fact, she wasn't sure it was exactly the same as her mother implied. She had heard of passionate ecstasies from older girls who read romance magazines, so she surmised it must be something very good. And this was, undoubtedly, very good. Except that it lasted longer than she had been told was humanly possible, and it occurred without stimulus or provocation. And, finally, it had a peculiar, and to her way of thinking, exclusive application in her case: it made her disappear.

"Now, when you say that, Helena," her mother continued, "you mean you can't see anyone or hear anyone?"

Helena bit her lip, shook her head. Why had she told? What had she expected?

"I can understand *your* part, but what do you mean they can't see *you?* I mean, *I* can see you. It hasn't ever happened around me. Has it?" She shivered; Helena rushed to speak.

"I don't know. I guess they can see me. But somehow, nobody ever asks questions while it's happening, and nobody needs anything from me. Nobody knocks me down or calls me on the phone. I think—that's what I don't . . ." She thrust her hands out, desperate. "Why don't they? Why not? Wouldn't you think they would? At least, once, in ten years? Doesn't it just stand to reason that every once in a while, when it's happening, somebody would need me or ask me, or—"

"But maybe it's a coincidence," her mother offered, wildly, hopefully. "Maybe this only happens when—"

"No, no," Helena said. "It doesn't. It happens anywhere. It has some power that keeps them from me. It happens in the middle of class or while we're at supper. Nobody *notices*. And I can't stop it once it starts."

Her mother reached for the hedge and steadied herself. It took a few moments for the questions to begin again. There was no going back.

"Then, you're saying it comes all at once?"

"No. I have some warning."

It happened at any time of day, though mostly at dusk. It could happen most intensely at dawn, when she was sliding from sleep to consciousness. It happened in every season, alone or in crowds, but it never seemed to happen in a loud place, or in a very busy place. The sensation itself was a combination of growing slowly warmer, while at the same time losing feeling in her feet, then her shins, knees, and on and on until, it was like . . .

"Like you must have felt when you were conceiving me." She had borrowed that language from health class, unaware it was the wrong one.

Her mother frowned. "Talk like a normal girl talks. Don't you *want* to be a normal girl?"

She did. But there was no use in that either. She had said as much as she knew to say, told as much as she understood to tell, and nothing had worked to the good.

Her mother had been too old to take the blow. A few more strikes at the hedge with the sheers and she quit, dragging the tool behind her as she went into the house to die. And die she did, two years later, after a long debilitating illness, a mysterious state of decline no one could pinpoint. She pitied Helena and gave her grave, futile looks from the bed, but she never blamed her. It was as though both of them knew that Helena was a scourge to herself, because both of them understood the strange nature of the power she had, and that in this inexplicable mode, how terrible a thing it could be.

Her father—never told, never understanding, consequently stupefied—had raised Helena the rest of the way. But her impression of herself had never waned. All through business college and into her first days as a teller at the bank, she hid her other failings. A tendency to forget on which side of the road to drive cropped up after a perverse driver-education teacher needled her with trick questions: "Before we pull onto the highway, are you *sure* we drive on the left?"

With some effort, she managed to convince herself that perhaps everyone had a secret passel of things to hide—and did hide. More reassuring was when Baxter had unwittingly revealed that there were pleasures, and then there were pleasures. The analogy between her private fits and marital bliss had been quite wrong. Nevertheless, the experience was terrible. The vanishings were somehow like pouring water onto the ground in front of a man dying of thirst—some mammoth cruelty, senseless in its waste, in its public privacy. For it, she would be punished. She should be. All she had would be stripped away when she was found out, when one day they saw she was not there.

That her diminished hearing might lead to her discovery was a deadening fear, so she had moved her desk around so that she looked out onto the bank lobby. Now she could see people advance down the dark marble floor well before they reached the carpeted section. No one could sneak up on her, mumbling as they came, and Stuart was a notorious mumbler. He talked into his papers as he shuffled them, making so much noise that it was impossible to hear what he said.

He was too young to be the manager, in Helena's view. Thirty-five and single and sporty, he paid too much attention to procuring the appearance of a Sears fashion model, and too much time involved in civic affairs. This Helena knew from the local newspaper, where he was regularly featured in "most eligible bachelor" sales for charities, and for hosting silent auctions to benefit popular diseases. He came to work at nine thirty, had a long lunch at eleven thirty, and left for something social at four. As Stuart rounded the ATM machine and headed for her cubicle, Helena stuck her hands behind her back and wiggled her fingertips.

"God Almighty," she understood him to say—not because she heard him exactly, but because he always started conversations that way. His black hair was freshly razor-cut, his suit, tightly fitted, his shoes, brightly shined. Helena could swear he wore clear lip-gloss. He stood at her desk, shuffling papers front to back to front again, as though they were out of order. Then he looked up from the shelf of his downturned brow and shook his head. Helena leaned in, straining to hear. She wouldn't need her fingers.

"Have you seen these?" he asked.

She gathered that he meant the figures from a report she'd done the Friday before. She swallowed hard at the possibility.

"Have I seen those?" she asked back.

He nodded. She nodded.

"So?"

"Yes?"

"Frauds."

She went a hard red from throat to forehead and stumbled to her feet. Her voice caught in mid-denial as the old threat scrolled rapidly through her head: *"First, you're fired . . ."*

"No! Not in the least! I've been here for thirty-three years and—"

"What?"

"Thirty-*four*—if you count the one that—"

"What?"

Helena shook all over: "I am not!"

He staggered, as though she might leap on him at any moment, and he would need a wider stance to take the blow.

"Not *what*, for God's sake?"

Helena swallowed. "What you said!"

He blinked. This time, he spoke up. "A *frog?*"

"A *frog?*" She sat down gracelessly and went hard red in reverse, from forehead to throat.

"No. Well, of course I'm not a *frog*. Certainly not."

Stuart's brow crinkled further. "I didn't. Why would I . . . why would I . . . ?"

One of her old tricks was not to let them focus too long on what she had given away. Diversions had to be huge and immediate. Shattered crystal vases could be forgotten if followed instantly by a fake heart attack.

"Those aren't the figures from the report, obviously," she began, "so there's no sense going down *that* road—"

"What road?"

"So what *is* that you have there? Let me see. You're hiding it. Is it? It is. It's a picture."

She reached for what he held and stepped around her desk toward him at the same time. Another distraction—invasive physical movement, abrupt and disconcerting. Plus, she could hear him better if she was right next to his mouth.

"Well. Yes. It's a picture," Stuart stammered.

Vertical green splotches springing from oval-like green splotches.

"Oh! Oh! Of frogs! A painting of frogs! Why do you have painted frogs?"

"They're . . . they're abstracts. For the auction. You *do* think they're frogs, then?"

"Oh, yes! Frogs! Certainly! Frogs on lily pads!"

She snatched all of the papers from his hand, a series of abstracts apparently downloaded from a computer. The next was a lizard, and then several chameleons. None were clear, and she could have easily mistaken them too, as Stuart had, if not for the hint he'd given. But she couldn't afford to draw his attention back to that misunderstanding. It was time for yet another tactic: exuberance.

"I love them!" Helena cried, clutching the papers to her chest. "So dramatic. So powerful. But reassuring. Comforting frogs. But dramatic. Are they yours? Who's the artist?"

Stuart shook his head. "I don't know. The name's in the e-mail. I just downloaded them from the museum and ran them off. I don't care which . . ." he stopped. "So you *haven't* seen them, then, like you said before?"

"Oh. No, I haven't. Did I get the e-mail?" She'd just gotten used to the old system when they'd upgraded it, so now she often deleted messages in attempts to open them.

"They're a sampling the curator wants us to choose from for the posters."

He might have said "poseurs." She hadn't been looking at his mouth when he spoke the word, distracted by her own flailing heartbeat. But since one mishearing was all she could risk, she only looked at him blankly. He rolled his eyes.

"The *posters*, for the art show. You said you'd handle that for me?"

"Oh! Yes, yes, yes. The benefit you're chairing. For, for what disease?"

Stuart shook his head. "It starts with a 'Q' I think. Makes you dizzy when you eat cheese. Or peanuts."

"That's a shame," said Helena. "Time something was done."

Stuart blinked again. For a time he was dangerously close to asking more questions, but Helena's exuberance, proximity, and volume, along with his own impending lunch date, gave him no time to pause. He was already ten feet down the carpet, with his iPhone out, fidgeting away.

"Well, anyway, there are the designs," he said, into his hands, trailing off as he walked. "You can meet with the curator anytime you want. As long as it's before next Monday."

She didn't catch the last part. Something about "ashlawns" and "monkeys."

Once back at her desk, she checked for the message. Ones from him were consistently marked "urgent" and written in all caps:

CONTACT PERPETUA BIRCH AT THE ART INSTITUTE. SHE'S A FRIEND. FIND 20-25 PAINTINGS. WE CAN'T SELL MORE THAN THAT IN ONE NIGHT. WHICHEVER SHE SUGGESTS, YOU SAY NO IF THEY ARE: A) SMUTTY B) STRANGE (THESE FROGS ARE AS FAR AS I'M WILLING TO GO) C) WORTH MORE THAN YOU CAN REASONABLY HOPE CARDIOLOGISTS AND DIVORCE

LAWYERS WOULD BUY, EVEN FOR CHARITY. GET LIZ AND JEFFERY TO COVER FOR YOU HERE. STUART.

Under other circumstances, she would have resented having to coordinate Stuart's charity duties. But she now knew there was nothing to fear from this responsibility. And she had no hesitation about giving her duties to others, since she hated and feared them so much. Like Stuart, Liz and Jeffrey were both young, and both were on the brink of being promoted over her. They had come as a brace, straight out of the same MBA, and had shot viciously up the ranks through all kinds of maneuverings, mostly having to do with their skills and determination and intelligence. Jeffrey could make Helena breathe hard every time he got out his calculator, all of the functions of which he knew how to toggle. He could even turn the display window an incandescent blue. Liz, his confederate, presented elaborate presentations using her laptop, and was forever pointing to things with a red laser pen, even to dropped pencils and pocket change. So when Helena left her tasks on their weekly "challenge lists," she had no regrets. Besides, they would only do the work faster and better than she, and this gave them the opportunity to show it. By mid-afternoon she was ready to call the art woman, and prepared for the conversation by looking through the pages Stuart had left her.

Frogs.

"What did you say?" The curator's voice was scratchy and coarse. She had a backwoods accent. Helena had turned the phone volume up full blast to hear. Passersby gave her murderous stares. But without a mouth to watch she was dependent on amplification.

"I said the *frogs*. He wants to use the frogs on the posters. And the invitations too."

"Oh. *That's* what you said. Well, all right. Do you mind if I ask why?"

Helena scrolled through Stuart's e-mail, still on her screen.

"He said the greens are pretty. Good for a spring event, like this is going to be. (He also said THEY'RE THE LEAST STRANGE.)"

Silence again. "What's an 'aspiring event?'" she asked.

Helena blinked. "I don't know." She was smart-alecky, this girl. It figured, being Stuart's friend.

"But you just said they were good for 'aspiring events.'"

"I . . . no, a *spring event*. This is going to be held in May, so—"

"Ohhh. Oh. A *spring event*. Yes. Green did you say? That's right?"

Not rude any longer. Quizzical. Unsure. Helena sat up. She squinted at a place on the carpet and listened to the girl's exuberance.

"We'll send you a mock-up." Her voice was faster. "Now the next thing is hammering out some details. I'm afraid it will have to be this weekend, though. So how about Saturday?"

Helena moved the phone away from her lips, placed a few fingers over the mouthpiece.

"Sunday at one."

"Monday at . . . noon?"

Helena smiled. "No. *Sunday* at *one*."

"Oh. *Sunday*. And at one. Wait. *Sunday?*"

"Yes. If that's all right?" She pressed her mouth hard against the phone now, and spoke loud at the girl. "My daughters have a birthday on Saturday," she winced, since she didn't really remember. "So, Sunday will have to be it."

At the end of the conversation she was even more pleased with her new duties. Two weeks away from Stuart, math, Liz, Jeffrey—plus, the curator was stone deaf. If only she disappeared intermittently on her way to hell, thought Helena, they might be good friends.

But her first impression was a bad one. The girl dressed like Liz, all in black and gray, with highlighted, blond-black hair, cut amazingly short. She was dumpy, even squat, and jangled all over with pewter jewelry. She had a broad face and close blue eyes behind severe horn-rims. Her mouth was small, to the point of a pucker. And the minute they made eye contact, Perpetua looked her up and down, glaring with the force of blunt shoves to the shoulder. Helena tried to overcome this initial shock. After all, they had something in common. She moved near and spoke in a loud, full voice.

"I'm . . . Helena . . . Brathwaite . . . from . . . the . . . bank. So . . . nice . . . to . . . meet . . . you."

Perpetua backed off, as though she had walked upon a mad dog.

"Why are you talking like that?" she asked; she all but sneered.

"Well. I—"

"This is a museum. Voices carry easily here. We have to keep from disturbing the patrons. Now, if you'll come with me, I'll show you the invitations."

Helena grimaced. She had even pulled her hair back, and shown her hearing aids more prominently just to put this girl at ease. She felt betrayed and decided to mumble. But her malevolence stopped cold when Perpetua asked her to tally up percentages for sales at the last five auctions. Helena pretended not to have brought the figures with her.

"What are those then?" asked Perpetua. She reached over and tugged twice, hard, at the manila folder under Helena's arm.

"What roses when?"

The girl shook her head. "No. I said: 'What . . . are . . . those . . . then?' Stuart said Liz had whipped up a spreadsheet. I assume that's what you've brought."

Helena smiled distractedly, feigned forgetfulness.

On the way to wherever Perpetua was taking her, they passed through long, drafty, marble-encased halls that opened onto galleries with lustrous wooden floors, smelling of fresh pine wax. Perpetua moved at a brave clip, barking out orders and reminders to whomever was close. Helena trailed along, looking at the faces of big men and women who responded obediently to the girl. And all the while the word "percentages" taunted her. She pulled out her calculator, found the "on" button, and pressed it—in case the thing needed to be warmed up. A solitary, squared-off "0" stared back at her, followed by a mean little ".".

Suddenly, Perpetua stopped at a spot in the wall that was padded with cloth, rather than fixed with marble. She pushed at a precise spot, clicking a spring that opened a hidden door. Helena stared at the magic, then at the girl who was motioning her inside.

"You'll need a quiet place to work this up. I have to oversee a hanging, so I'll leave you in here for about ten minutes."

Helena nodded, shuffled in. The door shut behind her like a rock rolled over a cave.

The dimly lit storage room was filled with stacks of boxes and tarp-covered tables. Signs that read "THIS GALLERY CLOSED" and "GIFT STORE THIS WAY →" stood lined in a battalion at one end. Helena slunk over to one of the boxes and sat.

In no time, she decided to invent a figure rather than persecute herself by attempting percentages. To her way of thinking, "$500.00" was about right. It was ten times what Stuart had sold for in one of those bachelor auctions. So she mashed in a "5" and two "0s" on the calculator and laid it on her lap.

At first, she just felt tired. The strain of the past day or so, the disappointment of not finding a kinswoman with poor auditory canals, and the nasty shock of percentages, had all taken their toll.

She leaned against the wall, closed her eyes, and let her stomach go in and out. Her girdle was too tight, so she shifted it about by moving her thumbs beneath the waistband.

It felt good, air touching her flesh, shooting down into places it had been kept from. In fact, it matched the stars that were now twinkling about her toenails, and alongside the bottom of her feet. Something like knuckles commenced to rub against her arches, softly undulating back and forth. A marmalade warmth oozed into her ankles, an orange glow that crept through her shin bones, then licked into the flats behind her knees, around her fat thighs, up and on, until . . .

"Oh. There you are."

Helena's head shot around. Perpetua was at the door, looking puzzled.

"Where were you? Did I lock the door behind me? I couldn't get in a minute ago."

Helena swallowed, her eyes darting about. "Clock on the floor?"

"'You . . . were . . . *gone,*' I said!" Perpetua walked her stout little body over. "You didn't answer before, and I couldn't get . . ." She stopped and stared at Helena. "What's been going on here?"

She was horrible. Helena had never experienced anyone like her. She demanded truthfulness as though she were her oldest, closest, most brutal relative—that, or a prison matron.

"Nothing," she stammered, childishly.

"Why are you lying?" snapped Perpetua. "You look flushed, or something."

"I'm . . . I'm hot."

"You're more than hot." She leaned over and sniffed Helena's breath.

"I have the number!" Helena whined, fumbling for the

calculator, holding it up for a distraction. But a line of digital zeroes filled the window from one end to the next. She must have been mashing it the whole time she was out. Helena dropped the calculator, and the threat began to scroll through her head: *"First, you're fired. You're not only fired . . ."*

For a time she cried, irrepressibly, and between heaving sobs managed to lie about why she was crying: her husband's brain condition, a tale pitifully but exuberantly told, with arms waving and hands grabbing at Perpetua's shoulder. But the girl would have none of it, which made Helena cry all the harder.

Perpetua got up, left, and came back with a cup of coffee. But she didn't hand it to Helena in a comforting way. Instead, she sat the cup next to her on the boxes and stood back to study her, as though she were drugging a convict for execution. Helena took a shaky sip as Perpetua demanded to know why she was carrying on like this, why she was so pathetically trying to disguise her deafness, why she looked like she'd just stepped out of a brothel, and who had told her to wear her hair like that.

Helena stammered out answers, but they were only partly true. She claimed she didn't like working for Stuart, that Liz and Jeffrey were more qualified and would have her fired soon, and that she wished she was as smart as Perpetua. Then she wouldn't have so much to fear.

The girl rolled her eyes. "How far are you willing to take these stories?"

"They're not all stories," Helen objected, chafed. "I *do* wish I was as smart as you are."

She thought she'd struck a sincere note, but Perpetua didn't thank her. Instead, she looked at the door, as though someone would knock on it at any moment. Then she let her gaze glide back to Helena.

"Look. I don't have a lot of time. But you're so obviously a wretch. So listen. I'm not—"

Helena sniffled. "Oh, yes you are. Stuart said so. And the way you order people around. They all listen." She motioned to the door and the people beyond it, then shook her head at Perpetua. "Do you have one of those light lasers?"

The girl glanced at her watch, then at Helena. She sighed again.

"I *am* smart. Of course I am. But I'm also ugly."

Helena set the coffee down, fearful of any spilling should the girl keep on saying startling things like that.

"No. You're not. You're—"

Perpetua sneered. "Yes I am. But I've turned it to my good. It's an advantage. You get to where you listen better because nobody wants to hear you talk. You don't have to be ugly to listen. But most people can't resist talking, if they're pretty enough."

It struck a sympathetic chord. Helena wanted to say so, but Perpetua kept on, a bit softer.

"All this listening has taken a toll on my ears."

Helena had to speak now, satisfied enough at the acknowledgment to return a little of the savageness she'd suffered. "Hearing aids will be awful," she said.

"Yes, but necessary."

"You could grow your hair out."

"No," said the girl. "I'll just have to watch more closely. We're good at that too."

Helena thought for a moment. "You mean—the ugly?"

"Yes. That's why I'm in art. I can see a great deal."

All of this talk was bizarre, but strangely interesting. The girl apparently had no qualms. "Why is that?" asked Helena.

"Because no one looks at me, I can look a bit longer myself."

This bolstered Helena's confidence. She rolled her shoulders and released her jaw muscles, settling in. But then, just as her relaxation had begun in full, the girl turned on her once more. She insisted on knowing where Helena had been and why she had been so hysterical.

Helena bolted upright. All the sawing back and forth had wrung her out. She couldn't move a step. Her nose was stuffed up, her throat ached, her eyes stung, and her stomach felt bare and fuzzy. On top of that, the girl looked mean enough to slap her if she lied. So for the first time since her mother, fifty years ago, she told. It didn't matter. This girl wouldn't die.

When she was done, Perpetua crossed her arms and scrunched her eyebrows together.

"How long does it last?" she asked.

"Three minutes and thirty-nine seconds," said Helena. "Forty-one, if it's night or raining."

Perpetua fired off questions like she'd been briefed with a white paper. Helena felt obliged to answer, and was surprised to find she could give them all so readily.

"Where do you go then? What is it like?"

"I float. But not physically."

"Not off your feet?"

"No."

"What part of you then?"

"The part behind my eyes."

"Go on."

"My eyes are open, but I can't see anything."

"Is it foggy?"

"Maybe."

"You can't say?"

"Yes, then. Foggy, but a bright fog. Not dreary. It's like being in a plane that's about to come out of a cloud."

"I thought you said it wasn't bright or dark?"

"I did, didn't I? And it's not either. But what I mean by *not* dark, well . . . I don't mean light has anything to do with it."

"No?"

"No. I mean *not dark* as in *not scary*—not frightening."

"But not happy?"

"Yes. Yes, happy but not—"

"Light."

"Yes. Not light."

"Or windy or still, either?"

Helena lowered her eyes. "You don't believe me."

"I didn't say that. I'm just filling in words when you get stuck. You've obviously never articulated this before."

"And these words are wrong, of course," said Helena. She wasn't reassured of the girl's belief, but she wanted to keep telling. "I never realized how much we use climate to talk about how things feel. Like it's either a trip to Florida or a trip to Alaska."

"Yes. But this isn't either of those things?"

"It isn't even a trip."

"But you do go somewhere?"

"I am somewhere. I'm just not exactly . . ." Helena stopped. "I sound like a witch with a Ouija board."

"No," said Perpetua. "They dress better than you do."

Helena glanced down at herself. "I used to dress better than this, before I had to—"

"Mmmhmm. Well, what's the problem? Why do you think it's so bad, so wasteful?"

"If I can't explain even the part about where I am, I sure can't explain that."

Perpetua grunted. "Yes, you can. Is it because you think it's obscene, that much joy?"

Helena shouted out loud, shocked. Precisely. A joy from expectancy, for what would be there when the cloud has come through. "But then it's all for nothing, and that seems—"

"Obscene," Perpetua supplied the term.

It took a moment to ask what she meant, because Helena was too pleased with the fresh diagnosis of her guilt. Perpetua rolled her eyes.

"I suppose it's possible—*possible*—that you have a great talent. To see. A larger capacity for splendor. Like levitators and nail-bed sitters. Because you're ugly too, you know."

Helena's mouth dropped, her joy gasified. This was too much. "I am *not*. How can you—"

"It's true."

There was no time for further offense. The museum was closing and Perpetua was in a rush to leave. But before they parted, she drilled Helena on her private history. She was reticent at first, but complied, thinking up answers to questions she had never really considered.

"I have to tell you, I have some doubts," said Perpetua. "But let me study this for a while. Let me see."

Over the weekend, Helena wondered about how the meeting had ended. She didn't know what she had expected to come from her confession, certainly not sympathy from someone like that. In fact, Perpetua had insulted her in a preposterous way, so hard fisted that it took a while for the sting to diffuse. It was still settling in when, as Baxter slept in front of a soccer game between Argentina and Papua New Guinea, the phone rang.

"Tell me more about your parents," demanded Perpetua. "What are they like?"

She could at least say "hello," Helena thought. The brusque treatment irked her, and she decided to return it.

"Dead. I'm sixty-five years old."

"*Were* like, then. Tell me. What did your father do?"

"He had a tire store. Never missed a day of work—not July Fourth, not Christmas Eve. You could set your watch by him. At night, he'd watch the news, eat chicken-fried steak—"

"Hobbies?" interrupted Perpetua.

"He liked baseball."

"Did he play?"

"No. Of course not. He watched it. He liked to garden—"

"But just tomatoes? Green beans?"

Ruder by the minute. "Yes. What does that mean?"

"All right. That's that. And your mother? Why was she always in bed?"

"Well, she was dying."

"*Before* that?" snapped the girl. "Stop being so literal. Any hobbies?"

"She played tennis once."

"She *did*? She *competed*?"

"No. She just played once. Somebody left a racquet at the Baptist church and they went outside against the wall—"

"All right," said Perpetua, vaguely contented. "That's enough. It's what I thought."

Helena lowered her voice; she glanced to see if Baxter was still sleeping. "What?"

"You've lived a pedestrian's life. From what I've gathered, the children you had in a haze of fear, and your husband and you have stumbled around each other your entire marriage, like thirteen-year-olds at a barn dance. Your job has been a curse ever since those qualified chicken-eaters died in the bus accident. You've gone nowhere, except to Pensacola in the summer, and six times to Clarksdale, Mississippi, to bury family. Your TV reception is poor, and your preference for polkas has kept you dry, musically. I've been through your drab little neighborhood. Finally, you have bad taste all the way around, which must make things even more baffling for your faculties."

Helena clutched the phone receiver, nearly bit the mouthpiece. "I have *not!* How dare—"

"Come now. Just look at yourself."

"I told you! This is what I wear because of the hearing aids—"

"Be honest. It wasn't any better before. You may think it was, but what do you know? Trust me. Your taste is horrendous."

It took several meetings before Helena could abide her. If it weren't for Stuart's constant questioning about the plans, and for the fact that she'd already told the girl too much, she would never have kept going to the museum. She felt like she'd gone to a loan shark and now couldn't shake her off. So, as the society ladies—who had always scared Helena, with their small ears and enormous eyes and expensive hair and polished smiles— planned the food and decorations at one end of the table, Perpetua and Helena sat at the other, planning the financial and artistic particulars. Rather, Perpetua planned and Helena nodded. She was increasingly angered at all the insults, and even skipped a session, suffering through Liz and Jeffrey's briefing on the gigantic strides they'd made in her absence. Out of desperation, she went back.

"What is it you meant by my 'faculty'?" she blurted out. Perpetua sat at her desk, drinking Coke from a mug and flipping through pages of an art inventory catalog. She looked up.

"I mean 'talent.'"

"It's not a *talent*," snapped Helena. How could anything that threatened her like this—with loss and death and damnation—be classified as a "talent"?

"It's amazing how little you know," Perpetua said, her gaze

descending again. "But I need to do a little more work before I try anything."

Helena bristled at the news. "Who said you were going to 'try' anything?"

"That's what you want, isn't it?"

She was silent. She didn't know.

"Why do you want to fix my 'talent,' then?" Helena asked, truly curious.

Perpetua turned the page. "Because that's one of mine."

After a few more days, the girl called Helena again, this time right before bed.

"I've got it all arranged. You have to come early tomorrow, before the gallery opens."

Helena was exhausted and didn't feel like getting up early, but Perpetua said she needed to test her theory. When she arrived, the girl was in a private, roped-off gallery. She was standing in front of a set of draped canvases on easels.

"I've wracked my brains and stared my eyes sore. But this is the best I can come up with. You've never been to a museum, have you?"

Helena scoffed. "Of course. To the agricultural museum, and to the Christmas museum. And that one with all the figurines from the plate company. I've even been *here* before, you'll be happy to know. I was in sixth grade."

"But you had no . . . experience?"

"Not that I recall." Helena looked about. "What's your theory?"

Perpetua grabbed her by the arm and dragged her before the first canvas, ripping off its covering sheet. Revealed was a field of blue bonnets at sun break. Helena smiled, reached out to touch the rich colors. Perpetua grabbed her arm and shuffled her to the next station. She tore the cover off again, leaving Helena before a stately Victorian woman with nearly all of her ample bosom exposed, and all of that dumping into a large, pressed-glass fruit bowl. Her eyes were black and her hair a vivid red. Helena smiled and commented on her figure. Perpetua clapped onto her wrist and dragged her down further still. The series played out: some cubists, some expressionists, some impressionists, a Photo-Realist, a Fauvist, and a Pointillist. Helena tried to touch each one, or talked of where she would display it in her home—over the fireplace or along the stair landing. But nothing happened.

"No. I didn't think so," said Perpetua. "They're not very good. But I'd hoped."

"Oh they *are*," smiled Helena. "They'll do fine. As long as they're not too expensive. Like I told you, only some professional people will be at this thing. So—"

"What? Oh. That. No. I was hoping you'd disappear."

Helena turned to look at her, head cocked to the side. "Why would I?"

Perpetua flicked her hand at the paintings. "Because I thought you might like one."

"I do. I do like them."

"Be quiet. You like them the way you like Cheetos. But that's as far as it gets."

Helena did in fact like Cheetos and turned her face to hide a blush.

"Why would you think I'd . . . have an experience . . . looking at these?"

Perpetua shrugged. "Because you sounded so disappointed when you described it the other day. Expectancies shattered, time after time. I figure you need something to attach this to. A reason for it. Isn't that what bothers you? That there's no reason?"

Helena thought for a moment. She could never answer her questions.

Perpetua nodded decisively. "You need a reason. No point in losing yourself into *nothing*. That's depressing as hell. You need a reason to be transported. This could be it."

Helena couldn't help blushing. "What could?"

"Beauty" answered Perpetua. "If I could only find some."

The girl bent to catch the end of a tarp and flipped it over the pointillist's sunset in Mauritania.

"No," said Helena. "I can't control when it happens. Even if I—"

"That's understandable," said Perpetua. "You'll just have to practice. You have to attach it. Force yourself. Have some self-control. Part of this is up to you."

"You sound like my mother," said Helena, looking away.

"She was right then, if she sounded like me. But you'll have to find the real thing. No pictures of it. The real object. Unqualified beauty. You've been so lazy, you'll have to have the full-throttled version to get you realigned. So you'll have to practice in the meantime."

Helena laughed. "I won't know how."

"Well, figure it out."

Bossy beyond belief, she thought, scowling. "What's it to you, anyhow?"

Perpetua scowled back "Because I want to *see* it. I told you. I'm good at that." And she straightened her ugly hair and walked away.

For the weeks before the showings, Perpetua brought Helena up to each picture, like a child taken to have her eyes checked. She stood the older woman before the pictures, then moved back to watch. She also explained who the artist was, what he was trying to achieve, why some people thought he had, why some thought he hadn't. Technical terms were thrown about—"sfumato" and "chiaroscuro" and "controposto"—though Perpetua warned, explicitly and repeatedly, that what they were after was more than any of those things alone. Helena listened and watched.

Nothing. Not even at the water lilies, or at the little girl with gardening implements, though she could now say why she liked the girl, but hated the implements. She could even use Italian to say why.

"So?" Helena asked, both frustrated and satisfied. Secretly at first, then more and more brazenly, she *liked* it that Perpetua hadn't figured her out. And she was *not* as ugly, *or* as badly dressed as she had said. Perpetua was headed into that same banished pile with Stuart, Liz, Jeffrey, her backdoor neighbor, her insurance salesman, and all the checkers at the grocery store. To make matters worse, the girl had the audacity to defend herself, and to even accuse Helena.

"It's *your* fault. I'm not saying we have any Botticellis here, but I'll be damned if I didn't think that little Dutch genre painting would've launched you. It seems to launch everybody. And I had to call in *big* chips and tell *big* lies to get it here for a day, just to show you. Your soul is *sooooo* flabby. You false-start like a gas lawn mower over something like the color of a blueberry ICEE, but when I show you *that* painting—"

Helena fairly quaked with wrath.

"I hated it! In fact, it was the ugliest thing I've ever seen in my entire life! The palette was all wrong, the light came from the wrong side, and the theme was about as ambitious as a picture on a Lite-Brite!"

Perpetua smirked. "You're getting petty, now. Turning on the doctor."

"Ha! The doctor! And just what have you done but talk big? Just 'listen' and 'look.' Well, all I've heard and all I've seen are *insults*. I was a fool to tell you. Just because you're *deaf!* I don't even want you to see it, now!"

The girl threw her head back. "Keep on. You just keep it up, here? Besides, if it really *does* happen, how come it doesn't happen to *me?*"

Helena was too mad to continue, and left without purse, coat, or umbrella.

It was raining hard outside when she got downstairs. Her car was parked a hundred yards away, and she'd have to go back to get her things. But her fury was glorious. She made a triumphant face at the streaked glass, took her hearing aids out of her ears, thrust them into one pocket and rifled through the other for cab fare. She didn't have enough and had to bum the rest from the docent. But once she'd hailed a cab, she relished at her storming out. It was for the best, because she didn't trust herself to drive on the right side of the road at the moment.

For days she feasted on her rage like a lioness, prowling about her house and yard. She tore out coupons only after the checker had tallied up her groceries. Twice she told bank customers she had no idea what they were talking about. For meanness, she threw the newspaper back at the paperboy. Baxter became wary and even let her watch the Ice Capades when Cuban boxers were on opposite. So when Perpetua had the nerve to leave a message a few days before the private showing, Helena raced to cut the machine off.

"Now, listen. I've found it. The real thing. It was sent for babysitting while they're preparing the exhibit space in Dallas. Call me as soon as you ge—"

Helena unplugged the machine in mid-voice. It wasn't the message, which she didn't catch half of anyhow (something about "babies" and "hippies" and "dolls"). It was that hick's voice she could no longer abide. The machine's red light flashed madly; the tape coughed and rewound and coughed again. But Helena only wrapped the cord in a hangman's knot around the body of the machine and left it to strangle. She wouldn't listen. She wouldn't call back.

But she wasn't allowed to stew in her satisfaction. With all her heart, she had wanted to leave Perpetua stranded out there, with whatever foolish enterprise she'd conjured up with the baby hippies. Stuart could take over now. In fact, the preview showing of the selected works, during a cocktail party for the society hostesses, would be right up his alley. However, when the evening rolled around, he had gotten a better offer: a fashion shoot in which the models were all young, successful executives. He broke his own record for leaving work early, not seven minutes after he had come in the door from lunch. Jeffrey was busy extrapolating logarithms for the bank president, and Liz was overhauling the inside of a Japanese database. Although only Helena was free, she would have refused if Stuart hadn't said that Perpetua would be with him.

"As a matter of fact, this shoot is her idea," he said, gathering his things, forcing his invitation into Helena's hand.

"Spur of the moment. It's to advertise a charity fashion show next month at the museum—held after hours, of course. So she's tagging along to oversee things. Doesn't really seem in character, but she insists. So you get to go hang out with the doctors' and lawyers' wives."

That night, Baxter couldn't be rooted out of his chair. So Helena forced herself into a black church dress with a white ruff at the collar and wrists, then put on some black shoes with white rhinestone buckles. Nice occasions required two layers of solid red lipstick and a glazing of face powder; she had gotten them free five years ago for trying out a new brand of shampoo. Then she drove herself downtown, late as it was. The cocktails would be over by the time she got there, and the showing might have already started.

So Perpetua wouldn't get the chance to see anything, Helena thought, smugly, as she surrendered the keys to the valet. What was the point, anyhow? Let them take the job and the house. The car was lousy. Baxter could watch cable at a motel. Maybe hell wouldn't be so hot.

But as she entered the museum lobby—its spare white marble polished and repolished, its plane-sized mobiles stirring gently beneath vent-blown zephyrs, its ebonized smells sharp in the thrilled, expectant air—she realized that she had not disappeared in quite some time: not, in fact, since she had begun hating Perpetua. She teemed with wrath, and like an animal with the taste of prey in her mouth, she was pulled down hall after hall by it, toward the place where the showings were to appear.

Along the corridors she passed, eyes sliding from frame to frame, sculpture to fountain to planter, her gait solemn and her shoulders high. The cooling night hugged against the skylights under which she walked, as though pressing itself inside. About and around were guards in blue uniforms, white-gloved waiters, and fifty-year-old woman after fifty-year-old woman, faces lifted to crowns, sheathed in silk and flounced in netting—speckled shoulders bare, wrists perfumed with lilac, throats chokered and garroted with fierce-colored stones. Helena needed no direction. She glided past them all.

In the center of a mammoth double doorway, weighted with cornice and pediment, stood an elegant, tuxedoed man, his silver hair swept back. He wore a pleasant, shrewd smile, like a bishop awaiting his flock's enfolding. He was the guide, Helena knew, and in his mouth and mind lay all the secrets of the walls and pedestals. She stopped in front of him and waited, her breathing strange and shallow.

Little by little, one by one, they all joined her—skirts sweeping the floor, tumblers and flutes dangling from emaciated hands, heavy with rings that scratched and clicked against the glasses. At length, the bishop smiled. He opened his mouth to reveal a brilliant red tongue.

"Wmmhsm," he began. Then, "wmmhmsml to za mmfdfdzz mmszm . . ."

Helena's eyes bulged. She moved closer, bumping a bare shoulder, jostling a fluted glass. But it was no use. Even with proximity, even with his gestures of face and hands, it was no use. In her apathy, in her rage, she had left her hearing aids at home, next to Baxter's remote control.

"La my wrzzzz?" he muttered, motioning to the room behind him. A jitter of laughter, smiles and nods of recognition. "Alrzzt. If u wlzfaaamuhme, wlz begnnz . . ."

And they all commenced to move, like sails across a bay, joining in twos and threes, streaming behind the bishop as he blessed them and led them into the vastness ahead.

Helena glanced around. No use. No use. The deaf could not follow the voiced, the lame could not follow the sound. She looked wearily about, to find her lost way back to the lobby.

They had seen her. She had put in a show. The bank, at least, could rest easy.

But before she could place the first step to leave, she spotted an elevated ledge, close to the gallery door. Free of all the dresses that had obscured it, she could now see that the surface held brochures, dreg-filled glasses, crumpled cocktail napkins—but also, to one end, a box of audio guides. She stepped closer.

Among the rows of black batons was one with her name taped to the earpiece. Helena picked up the guide, studied it for a moment, sniffed it, then carefully placed the thing to her ear and pressed the "play" button.

I was counting on your being the only one that would use these damn things, came the voice, *but I put your name on it just to make sure.*

Helena bridled and nearly spat. To pull this fraud, to go to these lengths, just to—

Now, shut up, said Perpetua. *There's not much time. Do as I say and I'll take you there. When you see it, even your flabby old soul will launch itself. It's hanging in the far room.*

Helena mashed the earpiece into her lobe until it pressed against the bone. Her vision blurred, went red. She could barely see to walk.

Who does she think she is, thinking she knows? Thinking she knows what it is—even worse—what *I* think it is?

But she could not make herself drop the guide, to stop the voice from ordering her about, for she was as curious as she was mad. The two things fought with each other, pushing the other forward, each a leg, moving past the other, again and again, in the way of her guide.

What does she think it is? My whole life I haven't known—and she thinks she knows. It's *my* talent, anyhow, so how does *she* know? With all her "perspective," "foreshortening," "elongation . . ."

I told him to take them through the impressionists first, to warm them up. The dresses love that. You have time to get ahead of them. Turn left right here, at the watercolor eggplants . . .

Helena turned left, and gritted her teeth until she felt the pressure in her gums.

. . . thinks she knows. With all her "tempera," "scumbling," "grisaille . . ."

Turn right again, and then a hard left at the taxidermy installation . . .

. . . with all her "controposto," "chiaroscuro," "sfumato . . ."

Push on now, just past the anonymous "Sun Breaking over Pacific." Push on, because they'll catch up with you soon. They can't be more than two rooms back . . .

And Helena could in fact make out a low, rich rumble behind her, heels upon hard wood, drumming like forces soon to breach a ridge. She swallowed, flushed. The light was dim here, through these rooms no one was meant to walk, on this path no one was meant to travel. It was a smoked light—a vague, clouded chasm. She dug the voice deeper into her ear.

Right now. And right again. Quickly.

The clamor behind her grew strong. The beats on the wood were matched by a high timbrel—drumsticks on drumsticks—chattering, chattering.

Ahead it lay, ahead and close, growing even now, a powerful bidding. And now her fury was leaving her, flying away and above her head. In its place came swift hunger and fleet thirst, a pulsing in her bones, a greed to move faster than she could. The air in her lungs surged past her ribs, sent bubbles through her veins, breaking through her skin. She was all water now, dammed at the top of a hill, the ocean far below.

You're near. You're near. Soon now. So soon.

The beats, high and low, became clinking wineglasses, tumblers of gin and tonic, stilettos on stained, waxed oak.

Listen. Watch. Listen. Watch.

And now their voices swelled above the beatings, coming from the room just behind:

"Look at the light! How much he does with light!"

"Yes. Yes. How well it's lit."

"How well the lighter lit the lighting."

Stop.

Like flags caught in a draft, the dresses—burgundy, saffron, ruby red, midnight blue—broke over the border, wave after wave, led into the room by their red-tongued, black-coated, silver-haired flame. They poured over the empty space, swirled about every surface, before every wall, in shadow and light, as though scouring out something they were sent to find. And their voices swung back and forth, from all about the room's borders, from every corner of its burnished wood frame:

"How the paint flows!"

"The reds! The blues!"

"Radiant."

"Luminous"

"Sparkling with inner fire!"

"It speaks to me," said one to another. "Does it speak to you?"

But Helena could not hear them, and they could not see her.

Perfect Silence

THEY ARE TELLING TONY that he cannot wear the clothes he is wearing. They surround him, just outside the men's locker room, and require that he step aside, so that others—dressed properly—can come and go.

Tony is short, slight, spectacled, with broad-set eyes. A downy mustache traces his top lip; swags of moppish hair graze his collarbones. They, on the other hand, are tall and wide-shouldered, with clean-shaven faces and bristle-tipped crew cuts. Tony is all in black: T-shirt, shorts, runner's watch; they are all in black too. He wears white running shoes with black stripes, as do they.

"But *Fitness* doesn't mean what it does on *your* shirts," Tony tries to explain. "I mean, it's something I *like,* not something I *do* for a living. It's something I aspire to. I want to *be* fit. I don't mean it like—"

"You can't wear it," says the larger of the two, a personal trainer.

"But I don't mean it like—"

"You can't wear it here." He steps around and stares at Tony's back.

"Did you have that made? Did you have that word put on the back of your shirt?"

Tony squirms. "Yeah. But I don't mean it like—"

The trainer steps around again, whispers hard in Tony's face.

"You shouldn't even be *wearing* a black T-shirt. *We* wear the black T-shirts."

The other, next to him, raises his hand, pats it in the air in a composing sort of way. He is the head trainer/weekday manager. His name is Jeremy.

"He's right. You can't wear that shirt, Tommy."

"Tony."

"You're causing confusion."

Tony smiles, shrugs. "But nobody thinks I'm really one of—"

"No. Nobody could think that," says Jeremy. "But there are other little people on staff here. The people who work at the front desk, for example. They're little. They might think you're one of them."

"But I wouldn't let them think that. I—"

The bigger trainer steps forward again. "Don't wear it, Tommy."

"Tony."

"Tommy."

"We *want* you to be a member of our club," says Jeremy. "But we have a lot of members already in this community. A lot of demand here. People are on the waiting list. So . . . you know . . . you *know*, don't you Tommy?"

Tony smiles a brittle smile. "Yes."

"All right. Now run take it off."

The two move further aside, to let a newly stomach-stapled man lumber out the door.

"But I don't have anything else to wear," says Tony.

"Better go on home then."

Tony's mouth drops. He points in yearning to the others, schooling about in the distance—where they are circling, twisting, racing, lifting.

"But I haven't worked out yet," he groans. "I haven't—"

"Can't be on the floor without a shirt, Tommy. Against fitness community rules. Run on home, now. Run on home."

★ ★ ★

THE TWENTY RIDING ELLIPTICAL MACHINES egg along to tunes from their headphones, chased by the twenty tromping on treadmills, the fifteen spinning on cycles, the ten climbing on stairs, and the five rowing on air. Other than the piped-in music—a rotation of power-pop and club-disco and hootchie rap—and a steady pounding on conveyor belts, a circular whizzing of gears, and an occasional clanking of metal plates on metal plates, all is as quiet as the ocean floor. There is little conversation: occasional low-volume exchanges, intermittent words of self-encouragement muttered as machines shift into higher levels of programmed difficulty—"Hills" . . . "Peaks"—or when one of the lifters strains his quads or pecs for a personal best.

The weights take up the other half of the club. A blue banner reading "STRENGTH," written in a hot gold courier, is suspended over the area, and signals the transition from the section devoted to "CARDIO," with its corresponding sign. The strength zone is itself split in half by mirrored panels: on one side, the weight machines, patronized by the old, the injured, the uninitiated; on the other side, the free weights, for those who have training theories and take eighty-dollar protein supplements.

Against one wall, separated from "STRENGTH" and "CARDIO," are three glassed-off rooms, each a chilled shade of black and blue. And behind the glass, silent as fish, the spin class rises onto peddles, to a beat and call meant for the riders' ears alone; next door, rows of seductive, midriff-bearing, pony-tailed girls stretch their legs, distend their spines, and shut their eyes in an Eastern peace; and finally, next to the yogis, a group of kick-jab-and-sway shadow boxers fight a furious fray with their own reflections in the dim, murky glass surrounding them on three sides.

6–10 M–F. 8–6 Weekends.

★ ★ ★

THEY ARE WALKING AWAY from the third guy, who still has one last set of shoulder presses on the bench. He cannot hear them; he has plugged his earphones back in, and selected his song on the iPod stuck in his beltline. Blazoned on his right shoulder, stretching down to his bicep, is an arabesque tattoo.

He begins to press. Air puffs into the space between his upper and lower lips as he strains, as though playing a trumpet. He cannot hear them.

"Dude. Let me get in front of you," says one to the other, looking behind him, laughing at their friend, who cannot hear.

The other smiles, ready to laugh. Then, suddenly, he does laugh—pleased that he's part of a conspiracy, a betrayal. He is huge, his arms bulging from a sweat-free jersey T-shirt that hangs far below his knee-length basketball shorts. His filthy ball cap is pulled low, so that his face is mostly the lower half, a grinning battalion of teeth. He is huge, but smaller than the other, who calls him "Dude." The other is mammoth, with even bigger arms and calves swelling from even larger clothing, but with no hat, and with a shock of curly black hair.

The two swagger toward the water fountain—their backs swollen like cobras, their lats shoving their arms forward from their sides as though they push invisible lawn mowers. Their friend, who cannot hear, who is being betrayed, is smaller than they by thirty pounds. He is big, but not huge; not mammoth.

"I don't want him to see. Dude. I don't want him to see me say this. Let me get in front of you."

"What? What?"

"Let me get in front of you!"

The other lets him pass, and he starts to laugh.

"What? What? You fucked her? Did you, man? Did you?"

"Man."

"Did you really? Oh, God!"

"Man, I fucked her right after she left his house! She came over and I fucked her."

He leans down, takes a drink from the water fountain, backs away, lifts the neck of his jersey to his lips and wipes his mouth on it. The other leans down and takes a sip, laughing too hard to swallow the water.

"But Dude. What kills me is . . . listen . . . Stop laughin' . . . Dude, stop laughin'! Stop laughin' or I'll kick your ass. Dude . . . just now, when he was saying that . . . about how she liked to rock around in the bed . . . how she liked to kinda rock herself to sleep after they . . . fucked—and he started laughin and I said . . . Dude, did you hear me? Dude, I said, 'Oh, I know . . . man that can go on for fifteeeeeen—'"

The other backs away, wipes his mouth on the heel of his hand.

"Dude! Nooooo!"

"Dude, I did! I did! I almost blurted it out—Christ!—I almost said it took her fifteen fuckin' minutes to settle down. I almost said it!"

"Dude! Noooooo!"

And their friend that cannot hear them drops his dumbbells,

cracks his bubble gum, holds his looks in the mirror, and sings the bridge of a Pearl Jam song that only he can hear.

★ ★ ★

Some of their T-shirts are vulgar; either suggestively— *Gardeners Do It in the Dirt; Long and Hard in Las Vegas*; or outright: *If you're close enough to read this, Eat Me!*

Some of their shirts show that they have somewhere, sometime, if not here and now, been on a "STAFF"—at a camp, at a hotel, at a clinic.

Tony sees the latter as he leaves to change for the second time and wonders why such a thing is allowed. He decides it's because "staff" does not mean what "fitness" does. Nothing means "fitness" but "fitness."

Some of their shirts state that they have given blood and encourage others to do the same.

Some have walked to stop cancer, or run to end heart disease, or biked to halt MS, MD, CF, AIDS, or SIDS.

Others have helped MADD, PETA, and DARE.

Some champion public television and public radio and public displays of the first amendment, and are answered by private hunting clubs and private golf courses and public displays of God.

Some advertise their work, some their banks, some their cell phones.

Others brag for bars and their beer, or shacks and their shellfish.

Some are devoted to schools, and the large cats and mean dogs that represent them.

Others memorialize a winning season played around one type of ball or another, and the designation of glory that was achieved thereby.

Fraternities and sororities.

Brand names and no names.

And clean white T-shirts that might be worn beneath dress shirts.

But only the trainers wear black.

★ ★ ★

They stop Tony again, right outside the locker room. They had not seen him reenter and are shaken that he has almost made it onto the floor wearing what he is wearing. He has on the same shorts and shoes. He also has on the same shirt, with "Fitness" written on the back, except that it's charcoal gray rather than black.

The big trainer spins Tony around toward the wall, as though he's about to frisk him.

"*What* are you doing?"

"It's not the same! It's not the same!"

"Take it off," says the trainer, who turns to the manager. "Make him take it off, Jeremy. Make him."

Jeremy nods, solemn and sad. "It's too close, Tommy."

Tony swings about. "It's not black! It cost me twelve dollars!"

"You can't wear gray," says the big trainer. "That's too close. I sometimes wear gray. Sometimes."

Tony ignores him, cranes his neck to see over his shoulder, "You said black! Jeremy—"

"He's right, Tommy. It's still too close."

The big trainer nods. "It could cause confusion, right Jeremy?"

He shoves a finger in Tony's face.

"Now, stop it . . . you just . . . you stop it. You can't be running around here in our clothes. You can't wear black or gray or white—not white either—don't you come back in here with a white shirt on and with that shit on the back. And change your shorts too. Make him change 'em, Jeremy."

Tony squirms free of the big trainer and dances close to Jeremy's side.

"You didn't say anything about that, Jeremy. You said—"

"You can wear black shorts, but you have to wear a primary or secondary-colored shirt. There're too many members, here. You'll cause confusion. We have to be able to tell each other apart."

Tony is downcast. At length, he looks up again.

"But I can wear black shorts and *these* shoes, right?"

Jeremy nods in beneficence. "Yes."

Tony glares at the big trainer, narrows his eyes.

"I can wear *black* shorts and *these* shoes."

THEY WILL NOT TALK TO HER.

She has tried for the last twenty minutes, and the boy behind the front desk has paged every one of the trainers on the floor. But no one will come.

She has everything she needs; she has cash, even; twice as much as they charge for a workout session. Still, they will not talk to her.

"Is this how it's done?" she asks, running her fingers through her cropped hair. It is straw-colored, but dull and thin and breaks off easily in her hand. Her cheeks are sunken and her collarbones jut up through her halter top like a sling blade.

"This *is* how it's done, isn't it? I ask for a trainer and someone's supposed to come here and meet me and we settle on a workout time, right?"

"Yes," says the pimply boy behind the desk, but he is looking at the crossword in his lap. He has done nearly all of the "Down" but none of the "Across."

She sets her half-liter water bottle on the counter and pulls her tights up over her rock-sharp hip bones.

She weighs eighty-six pounds today. She is fatter than she has been in a month, before they made her come home for a visit. There was nowhere to work out there, and no one would have let her go even if there had been. So, as soon as she got off the plane, before she even went home, she came here to begin. She changed into her workout clothes in the airport bathroom, then got off the subway five blocks from the gym so that she could walk the rest, to get her lazy metabolism restarted. She rolled her carry-on luggage behind her, all the way uphill from the station.

She feels better, for having done that.

The activity swimming around without her makes her anxious. She lowers her head to catch the boy's gaze, to make him look up from the puzzle.

"That's the way it was done before, I mean. That's the way it was always done."

The boy picks up the phone. "Jeremy to the front desk, please. Jeremy to the front desk."

She leaves her luggage standing upright next to the counter and moves out onto the floor, wading into the "CARDIO" section as she searches for someone to talk to her. She hobbles on her blue, calf-length cast boot, meant to knit together her shin, which is said to be fragile and easily shattered.

One of the black-clad trainers draws close; she reaches for his shirt, tugs at his sleeve.

"Can you work me out? I have all afternoon."

He shakes his head. "I'm with a client."

"I can wait."

He moves away, "I'm full today."

"Tomorrow?"

But he walks on and shuts the glass door to the office he enters. She hobbles back to the desk.

"I don't understand. This is *really* too much. This is your business, isn't it? I mean, you want people to buy sessions, don't you? It's on all of the posters in here—*Buy Workout Sessions!*—And I have cash. Is it a matter of—"

The boy turns on the speaker again, talks as he enters a four-letter word into the boxes for "six across."

"Mitchell to the front desk, please. Mitchell to the front desk."

She holds her breath, searches the floor in hope.

"Which one is . . . oh, here he is. Excuse me. *Excuse me*—"

But he pulls out his cell phone and starts to speak as he passes her by.

She spins around, glaring at the boy.

"He didn't even stop. I don't—"

"Monica to the front desk, please. Monica to the front desk."

"No," she says, shaking her head. "Not her. I don't want a . . . just call . . . call Mitchell again. Or Jeremy. Or Stuart? Is he here? Stuart? Or Jared?"

"Everybody's busy," says the boy.

She sighs. "Is there a class, then? Spin? Step? Pilates? Anything?"

The boy looks up, checks the schedule, "Yes. In about fifteen—"

Jeremy has stolen up behind her and is making a sawing motion across his throat, so that only the boy can see it.

"Buuuut—it's full," he says, as Jeremy steals away.

She sighs again.

"I'll wait, then. I'll wait . . . on the treadmill."

★ ★ ★

TRAINING SESSIONS ARE CONDUCTED by credentialed professionals—certified, conscientious, safe, discreet.

They know how to potentialize dreams, maximize effort, emphasize results, and realize goals, whatever those goals may be: from beach bodies to buff brides, from power punchers to pyramid peakers, from marathoners who bust through walls, to mommythoners who takes back figures.

Just consider the possibilities: the return of stamina once enjoyed, the achievement of targets never known, the realization of grace, the attainment of might, stature, presence.

The only thing standing between you and success is commitment and know-how.

If you commit, we know how.

We're excited about your mission.

We want to be part of your reaching it.

So join us.

We want to join you.

Why?

Because *you* are the point of *us*.

Sessions are available singly or in packs of eight at a reduced price.

Sessions are non-refundable . . .

Non-transferable . . .

And must be used within ten weeks of purchase.

Join us.

★ ★ ★

THE MERELY BIG GUY is in the shower. He is standing with his weight on one foot, his hands against the tile, his head bowed, allowing the jet of water to pulse and thrash between his shoulder blades. He cannot get the Pearl Jam song out of his brain, and is humming it as he imagines himself in the evening to come: his shirt tight against his physique as he walks through a halogen-lit bar. His spray tan glows; his chemically whitened teeth shine. The girls do not look until he passes, but when he passes, they look for a long time. He will wear his white cotton pants and his leather sandals and his blue knit-shirt and . . .

"Dude," says the mammoth guy. He is at the bank of sinks, shaving his throat as he looks in the mirror.

"What?" says the huge guy, next to him, shaving his shoulders.

"You'll be at the party tomorrow, right?"

"Yeah."

The huge guy looks at the mammoth guy's reflection, then motions with his head to the showers.

"Is *he* coming?" he asks, in a low voice.

"I don't know," says the mammoth guy. "I'll ask him tonight."

The huge guy flicks the lather off his razor into the sink.

"Or you could ask *her* tonight."

The mammoth guy snorts.

"Dude. Shut up."

"Seriously. Seriously. Are you? Again?"

"What?"

"Ha ha ha ha."

"Dude? What? What?" The mammoth guy leans down and splashes his face, laughs.

"You know! You know!" says the huge guy. "You are, aren't you? Tonight?"

"Dude, shut up."

"'Rock-a-bye Baby,' Man!"

"Dude, Shut up! I'll kick your ass. Seriously."

"Ha ha ha ha ha."

"Dude, shut the fuck up. He'll . . . ha ha ha ha . . . he'll hear you."

"Ha ha ha ha—No, he won't."

The merely big guy in the shower shuts off the tap and shakes the glistening water from his hair. The droplets spin away like a shattered crown. He reaches outside the curtain for his towel and hums as he scrubs himself dry.

There is a book in his case. He bought it one day because the color of the cover matched his bag, and the color of the bag matched his shirt, and the color of his shirt matched his pants, and the color of his pants matched . . .

"Dude?" says the mammoth guy, in a softer voice.

"Yeah?" laughs the other, softer still. "Are you?"

★ ★ ★

THEY HAVE STOPPED TONY AGAIN, just outside the lockers. They have stopped him despite his permission to wear black shorts, despite his sanction to wear white and black striped shoes, despite his obedience in the primacy of his primary-colored shirt: bright blue with red piping at the sleeve cuffs and neck. They have stopped him again, spun him around, and this time objected to his choice of words:

IMN2Fitness

"You said it was the color! It's blue! I'm wearing blue! Jeremy, you *said*. You *said!*"

Jeremy hugs a clipboard to his chest. The big trainer steps back, seething, pacing about, as though he doesn't trust himself.

"Well," says Jeremy. "Now that I think about it, it's not. It's not just the color after all. That won't do either, what you've got written on there."

"'Fitness' is *our* word," snaps the trainer.

Jeremy thinks for a moment, his upper teeth biting his lower lip. He looks at the clipboard, takes out his pen and sketches something down, then tilts his head to assess it at a different angle. At length, he nods.

"You can use 'Wellness.' 'Wellness' is your word. 'Fitness' is ours. We're 'fit.' You're . . . well—"

"Not for long," says the big trainer, jerking his chin at Tony. "Not if you keep pulling this shit. I swear to God. Not if you—"

Tony ignores him, presents a hurt face to Jeremy.

"But that's not . . . nobody would . . . that's not the *same*. I want—"

"To be the same as us!" says the trainer. "See? See?" He *admits* it! You *admit* it!

Tony looks about. There is no color that will do, no word that is adequate, no combination that will suffice. All other ways foreclosed; all other paths denied.

"What if I get a job here?" he asks.

Jeremy frowns.

"What?"

"At the reception desk. They're . . . they get to wear the shirts, don't they?"

Jeremy nods. "Yes."

"Well?"

The big trainer jumps in, "We don't have an opening, do we?"

Jeremy shakes his head, "No. Not right now. Not there, at least."

The big trainer smirks, "Oh. Yeah. With the cleaning staff, though. You could work with Jorge and Bonita and Juan Miguel and Ishtar. Is *that* what you want, *Tommy?*"

Tony's gaze unmoors, drifts about the calm, hushed, moist fury before him.

"Do they get to work out?" he asks.

The big trainer's smile drops from his face.

"Of course," says Jeremy, "in off-peak hours. They're part of our community."

★ ★ ★

S HE WANTS THE TREADMILL. She has already switched from the rowing machine to the bike, which were both too easy. True, she couldn't manage the Stairmaster. Yet. But she figures if she walks at an even pace on the conveyor belt, the boot won't get in the way too much. In fact, she's glad she has the boot, as it's harder with it on, and she feels she'll get a better workout this way. But she really needs the treadmill.

She would never use the elliptical. Not unless there's nothing left, and even then she would only use it going backward and without placing her hands on the poles.

"It's too easy unless you do that," she heard a trainer say once, back when she could get a trainer to work with her. Now they're all "too busy."

The truth is, she knows full well, that they only *want* to work out fat people—people who *like* being fat, and don't know *how* to work out, and don't really *want* to—people who quit after twenty or thirty slack dog minutes. That way it's easier for the trainers and they can make more money. They don't want to work out someone like her, who knows what she's doing and can tell them when they aren't working her hard enough.

She stands next to a girl who has been on the treadmill for twenty-six minutes—which she knows because she timed her while she was on the bike. She's been watching this girl, sure that she'll try to take more time than she's allowed, although the signs clearly say *Thirty Minutes on All Cardio Equipment During Peak Hours*. And these are peak hours. She's been watching her closely.

She should have gotten off the bike when one of the treadmills became available earlier, but she was in the middle of a *cardio-blast* cycle and didn't want to stop. But she should have, because now all the treadmills are taken, and this girl, whom she knows has been on the longest, is planning to stay longer than she should. She couldn't blame her, what with her fat thighs and fat rump and fat face. She could probably stay on it all day and not lose a pound. Even the looks of the girl make her sick, make her regret the yogurt and apples and cantaloupe her mother had made her eat before she left.

She paces in a circle around the girl, staring. But the girl keeps her eyes on the television monitor, acting like she can't see her or hear her beyond the headphones.

She looks at her watch. Twenty-seven minutes and forty-eight seconds.

When it's time, she'll tell her. Yes sir, she will have *no* problem telling her that time is up.

She paces back and forth, avoiding her reflection in the mirrors, looking away when she catches it.

She wants a different form, shape—the right one, the proper one. And she wants to know if she's doing it correctly. If she is apt. She'll do the work. She just needs someone to tell her she is doing it right, doing it well.

But they won't talk to her. They're too busy talking to each other.

And she cannot hear Jeremy tell the boy behind the counter not to let anyone take her, that he has e-mailed everyone about her particularly—and about all people like her generally—to make sure that no one takes her on. No matter how long she stays . . .

"We can't be a part of something like that," says Jeremy.

Twenty-nine minutes and fifteen seconds, sixteen seconds, seventeen . . .

★ ★ ★

THEY ARE SUITED. They have pulled on their slacks, buttoned their starched shirts, belted their waists, tied their cravats, slipped on their jackets, socked and shiny shoed their feet, splashed their faces with sharp cologne, and are now suited for the rest of the afternoon.

The suits don't fit them well, though; they are awkward and inelegant, like bulls in fine harness. But it won't be long now. In a few hours, they can don their tomcat clothes to which they are better matched.

They take the flight of metal stairs that lead up from the blue and black floor to the light of day.

The merely big guy is behind them. He has his iPod in his jacket pocket and has the plugs back in his ears. He looks slimmer, better in his suit than the mammoth guy or the huge guy, because he is merely big. He is replaying the Pearl Jam download.

Their feet clank on the steps like rocks hitting a diving bell.

"Who are you bringing?" asks the huge guy.

The mammoth guy looks over, "What?"

"Tomorrow, to the party. Who are you bringing?"

"I don't know," shrugs the mammoth guy. "Who are you bringing?"

"I don't know."

They turn the flight of steps, ever closer to the surface.

"Yeah you do," says the mammoth guy. "You're bringing Christy."

"No. I don't know. I may not. But you're bringing Caitlyn."

"No. I'm not bringing Caitlyn." The mammoth guy thinks for a minute. "Have you seen Caitlyn?"

"No. Why?"

"I just wondered."

The huge guy thinks for a moment. "Have you seen Christy?"

"Why?"

"Just wondered. Have you seen her?"

The mammoth guy shrugs, smiles, more to himself than at his friend.

"Only when I saw her with you."

The blue tinted glass door opens. They enter the warm, wet air, and the merely big guy behind them breaks into a song, his eyes closed, his face twisted in pleasure.

"Can't tooouuuuch the bottoooom. Innnn tooo deeeeeeep. Yeah . . . yeah . . . yeah . . ."

★ ★ ★

TONY REENTERS THE FLOOR in his black shorts, his white shoes with black stripes, his black runner's watch, and his new black shirt with *Fitness* on the back. He has to wear a white cap too, and white gloves, and a short white apron, and carry a cleaning agent and rag.

But the word is clearly on his back. This time, no one stops him.

It is very quiet now, as most have re-suited themselves, ascended back to their lives on the surface. There are only a few old people left, who continue to school about in one area or the other, and one grotesquely skinny girl in a boot cast, who's trying to make the treadmill incline higher than it can. The quiet is still and deep. When a sound is made, it echoes in a fathomless, muted way that would travel far into the cockles of the ear, if anyone were listening.

Tony swims his way through the reefs of equipment and slips up beside Juan Miguel. He is a short, fat old man with a puckered face. He is spraying down the treadmill bases and wiping off the dried sweat.

"How are you?" asks Tony, ready to spray and wipe, spray and wipe.

Juan Miguel shakes his head as he works, *"No comprende. No hablo inglés."*

"Me?" asks Tony, smiling, spraying. "I'm well. I'm well."

In Lieu of Flowers

ELEANOR DRAWS HER SWEATER about her shoulders.

Despite the sultriness of the floral shop, she is always chilled and wears a thin pastel drape over her sundress.

Her employees, back when she had many of them, used to hint at how hot she kept the place. But now that she has only the part-time girl in the afternoon, and the delivery boy she shares with the cleaners next door, she doesn't have so many complaints to disregard.

Demi-moon reading glasses rest on the end of her nose as she stares at a set of unpaid invoices.

Nothing can be done about them until her oldest son in Charlotte talks to the banker and tells her youngest son in Atlanta what to do with the funds. The only help they can give her now, at this distance from home, is to manage her finances. One is a lawyer, the other a broker, and between them they move money about in her accounts so that they only reach practical depletion at the end of every week.

It's a careful game, she's been told. The balances rise and recede, and they must watch them like a cardiogram, waiting for an erratic spike or trough.

Eleanor puts away the invoices, rests the glasses on the top of her head, smoothes her gray-black hair and adjusts the abalone combs that hold her bun in place. Then she eyes the front door, which she'd unlocked for the first customer over an hour ago.

The slope that brought her to this financial chasm has been gradual but steady. It was noticeable from the outset, in fact, like an angle of descent felt in the bottom of the feet, though for all intents and purposes the surrounding landscape appeared quite level. She'd sensed it coming, perceived it happening.

And she can blame it all on charity.

It could be borne at first, these newfound channels of philanthropy. She'd noticed when the obituaries, which she read daily to mark down the principles concerned, announced that *"in lieu of flowers, the family requests that a donation in Mr. Hillenbrand's name be made to the American Heart Association"* . . . *"in lieu of flowers, the family asks that gifts be made to the scholarship fund set up in Mrs. Winchester's name"*—and on and on and on.

She'd lingered over such announcements when they first appeared, looking for some portent of the future—a weak spot in a stone wall, a fissure slipping a hollow knife into the edifice, cleaving it with an invisible power.

But business had been good at the time. Back then, she'd had two locations and seven employees. With plenty of customers, her reputation as the florist of choice kept her prices high. Plus, the trend was slow to develop. Even now that things have changed, some still share her view. You can't stop the Catholics from having masses said for the dead but they'll send flowers too; they don't make it an either/or proposition like the Methodists and the Presbyterians. The Baptists buy flowers better than anybody, though. They never slight custom, which is why she maintains a nominal membership.

Still, as the traditionally minded age, she expects further sufferance. Trends are more keenly felt in a town of middling size. Considering that people die all the time, even if they get married with grocery store bouquets, the overall decline in flower-giving is constant. Worse, the sick have become unreliable, what with insurance companies rushing them out of hospitals before there's time to send anything.

And while babies have always been a staple, the Mylar balloon business—which she can't make herself touch, yet—cuts into that market.

Anniversaries have been weakened by the dirty underwear trade, as has Valentines, which was always a one-off shared with the chocolatiers.

And then the rash of home gardeners and farmers' markets take their share. In the past, any decent woman would cater a party and have a florist do the centerpiece, not grow it all herself, sweaty-faced and grubby-handed.

The clock ticks. The door chime rings.

Eleanor looks up, guarded in her hopes. Her face falls.

It is only the part-time girl, Afton.

In her fitted sheath, Afton is tiny-waisted, big-breasted, and round-bottomed—a milkmaid come to town. The whole strategized endeavor of her figure is crowned with an aura of corn-yellow hair framing a dimpled, painted face.

"You used the front door?" Eleanor asks.

"The back was locked," answers the girl.

Eleanor frowns at herself.

"I guess it slipped my mind."

Afton moves through the shop toward the work room, her caustic perfume suffusing the air like crop dust.

"That's why I had to come in the front last Wednesday, too. And last Monday."

"Where are you going?" Eleanor asks.

The girl swivels on one foot.

"To put my yogurt in the refrigerator."

Eleanor nods.

"I'm sorry you had to come in so early. But I guess you'll have to eat right now since you can't have it up here at the counter when I'm gone."

Afton blinks.

"It's ten forty-five in the morning."

"I know."

"Your luncheon's not 'til twelve."

Eleanor gives her a stiff smile.

"But I have to leave at eleven fifteen today. I'm in charge of the speaker and I have some errands to run. You have time, though. Go ahead—while I'm still here. Let me move my things."

If she doesn't watch her, Afton might leave the counter unattended. Times are hard enough without it looking like the shop is empty.

The girl sits at the stool behind the desk and eats in a desultory way. She will only have half of the yogurt anyhow. She's losing weight for a pageant, one she's qualified for by winning a local competition.

You couldn't expect a refined girl to work afternoons. There's something too arched in the way Afton stands—a result of being trained to pivot and show the curve of her buttocks. But she pays attention to her appearance, and Eleanor has to have her.

Before she leaves, she decides to inspect a vase of sky blue hydrangeas, which will serve as the floral accent on the speaker's dais. It's a big showy variety, a statement piece. The drowsy heads droop like young children, beautiful in their slumber. Eleanor hopes to land some bridesmaid's luncheons and baby showers with it—to the degree girls these days order anything nice for the table; to the degree girls these days even bother with a table; to the degree girls these days ever marry and have babies.

Afton takes another bite, pushes the yogurt away and begins to stare into the glass countertop to check her lipstick.

"I passed the new park on the way," she says, running a finger along her teeth.

"The 'Nature Preserve,' they call it," says Eleanor.

She turns each hydrangea leaf over, one by one, as though checking a baby's ears.

"Well, they were putting in a tree up front, near the entrance."

"Who was?" asks Eleanor, absently.

"The third grade. At least I think it was the third grade, because I recognized some of them. I visited there last month to teach them how to brush their teeth."

She sighs.

"Try brushing your teeth with a crown on your head."

Afton is always telling Eleanor how hard her life as a beauty queen is; she was nearly kicked in the chest by a mule last month, handing out ribbons at a livestock fair.

"Why was the third grade putting in a tree?" asks Eleanor, satisfied with the hydrangea's health.

"It's a service project. The teacher said they come across the street from the school and help plant them. You know. Kind of an education thing—digging and sticking things in the ground and covering them up with dirt. You know. Education. Takes up a whole morning."

"Planting trees?"

"Well, they're supposed to be helping. The men at the place really do it, but the kids kick dirt in and get their picture taken. Beside the marker."

Eleanor flinches.

"What marker?"

"The marker in whoever's memory it's in. You know. For when somebody dies, and the family donates a tree or something to the park. It's a project they started. The teacher told me."

Eleanor stiffens.

"*Who* started it? The memorials—who started that?"

Afton shrugs.

"The park, I guess—the 'Nature Preserve.' But not just trees. People can give flower beds and water features and even some big boulders. It's something they do now instead of—"

Eleanor cuts her eyes at the girl.

Afton turns back to the yogurt.

"I'll be back at two," Eleanor says and picks up the hydrangea.

She has a hard time staying in her lane as she drives toward the country club. People honk as she drifts toward oncoming traffic.

This news would come today—of course it would—right before her sons tell her whether she's finally sunk into the red too far to climb out again. So on top of the other charities robbing her of business, now all of nature has set itself against her. They've joined league, in fact—charity and nature, in a tandem assault.

And this she never saw coming; this new front supplants her altogether, using her own means of survival as the attack weapon. Instead of buying flowers in honor of the dead, people can plant live ones for the same purpose—a living monument—and with a marker that identifies the donor. Better yet, a whole tree or an entire forest could be given—depending upon the level of affection.

Naturally, the preserve would put it in those terms: the old ratio of love to expense, compounded by grief. She knows it well.

But the coup de grâce: to use children, exploiting them in this transparent ploy, a maudlin chain between those beginning life and those ending it.

She has to admire the genius.

Eleanor slows to a pace ten miles beneath the speed limit. She is oblivious to lights turning red and green, running through the former and stopping at the latter.

Further still, they've beaten her to the punch. She'd planned an entire marketing campaign around a tactic she'd learned of: Green-timidation.

The idea was to bully and browbeat and guilt-foist the whole town with the biodegradability of her trade as opposed to the carbon indestructibility of other gifts. Like temperance leaguers and suffragettes, righteous women with organic, hemp grocery bags would have jumped at something put in such terms.

But now the Nature Preserve has gone her one better: Why give dead things when you can give living ones? Why destroy nature when you can work within it?

Eleanor looks over at the pot of hydrangeas riding in the floorboard of her car. Their heads bob in scentless, sky blue mockery.

On the way to the club, she stops off at the car parts store to buy oil. The light has been on for a month and she smells metal smolder when she drives. She'll have to cajole her neighbor into changing it for free, flirting with the old man enough to get it done without making his wife mad. The disgusting diplomacies of her impoverished existence keep her in a perpetual cycle of drawing back in revulsion even as she pushes forward through necessity.

She turns onto the road, drifting onto the shoulder at times, driving cyclists into hedges.

For the first time in years, she misses her late husband, Max.

An unscrupulous speculator, Max would have responded in kind to the Nature Preserve's tactics. Not one tree would have been left standing, if he'd had anything to do with it.

The thought both exhilarates and terrifies her, as anything related to Max is prone to do.

He'd been a very good crook, Max had—a fact she'd suspected but left unverified out of self-defense. His infidelity in every other aspect of their lives had been confirmation enough. Deceit had been an ineluctable mode with him, as natural as a wolf's campaign for meat. In equal parts furtive and strong, his method could even make his targets complicit in their undoing. He charmed a familiarity from them that first lowered their guards and then brought them within the reach of his danger.

Eleanor swallows hard at the thought.

It wasn't until after she'd married Max that she realized all of this, along with the unsettling suspicion that such a thing was exactly what had happened to her. From an established family of estimable renown, if no longer considerable worth, she was later, much later, confirmed in that fear.

Regardless, she'd stayed married to him for many reasons: because he'd amazed and awed her; because she'd been afraid to leave him; but mostly because she'd known his prowess would provide—the way the weaker members of a pack could always feed upon the leavings of the stronger. So she'd lived her life courting both his favor and his neglect—hoping to be forgotten, for safety's sake, but preparing to be worthy, if notice came. Until the end, it had been a risky but profitable existence, one she was never sure if she was cleverly negotiating or foolishly perpetuating. What seemed progress with him could just have easily been a circle; what seemed peace, only chloroform.

She glances at the dashboard clock. There is still time for a few more "errands"—a word that is now collapsed in meaning for her—signifying either payment of money she does not have or the forestalling of debts she cannot abate.

Gunning the engine, she speeds on.

Unlike Max's kind of dishonesty, for which she'd had no talent, her own strategy has been of a different composition, though also made from his leavings.

Where Max had whispered "love eternal," then flashed a thin stiletto, she has cried "love lost," then shaken a tin cup.

Of course, she has provided the finest flowers for her patrons, all tastefully arranged. But more importantly, she has provided the satisfaction that comes with supporting a woman of good breeding, of impeccable standards, who has suffered greatly but soldiered on; a woman who has been through the wars—is still fighting them, in fact—but does so with a high-held head, a stiff spine, and a bright, tearless eye.

She has given her patrons their money's worth, wrapped in a pure white stole of virtue.

When Max had fallen so devastatingly ill, and had lingered so incredibly long, her sons were still in college. And without his shrewdness to know what deals to make, without his ferocity to know what debtors to hound, without his craft to know what creditors to avoid, the money had dwindled fast.

The whole town had witnessed her assumption of a struggling floral shop that Max had foreclosed upon—the only one she could step into the daily operations of with some semblance of decorum.

Publicly, she'd borne all, even as Max lay stricken, drooling, walleyed, and incontinent—though hardly powerless—at the total care facility whose daily cost had bled them white. It was years before he'd died and years yet before the business was a going concern.

She turns into the post office to mail minimum payments on her credit accounts. There is no equity left in her home because of the second mortgage needed for financing; if her sons call with bad news today, she won't be able to pay the house note again.

She slides the envelopes into the drop box and waits for a moment, considering the possibility of public sale.

Do such things really happen? she wonders. From the courthouse steps?

She also wonders what use such a loss will be—what gain can be enjoyed from fortune's slights if her business is already gone?

Pity is wasted when all hope is past.

Stirring herself, she shifts the car into gear and pulls back onto the road.

Without Max, she's had to draw upon her former circle of acquaintances for benefaction. And a large part of her success has lain in knowing their proclivities. They have an affinity for public dignity, something that she shares, coupled with a penchant for public empathy, something that she does not.

Regardless, knowing this she has fashioned a matron's persona for them, one of valorous proportions—an ancient statue retrieved from some cave in Rome, some ditch in Pompeii—an empress honored as much for the indignities she's suffered as for the station from which she came. Her marble cheek, stained by water and sullied by grime, shines through life's assaults with a bearing that defies them. And those that circle about her behold this unassailability, born from a holy spring, somewhere deep within.

All note. All hail.

In return, the world at large could witness the purity of her congregants' souls. In short, they are ennobled by the comfort they pay her, the quiet dignity of the intimate court they keep.

The beneficiary of their largesse is a reflection upon them, a credit to them, a blessing for them.

All note. All hail.

It had worked for a long time.

But right when things were settling into place, the politicians had gone and ruined the country. Rome was sacked again; Pompeii, smothered once more.

And now she is not alone in bearing the assault of grime and the sully of a fallen estate. Worth is dissociated from name, has become confused with net worth, as it is historically wont to do. She is not as noticeable when none are hale and fit. As broken as they are broke, the circle has shattered. Their eyes have turned inward, toward their own wounds; now, none can see hers; worse, none cares to see.

So she finds herself trapped, her patronage waning, with her only support a product that the media constantly characterizes as a "luxury" purchase, and facing an ever-growing phenomenon in which there are new options, abundant alternatives, "other, more permanent ways" to show affection in lieu of the only damn one that keeps her alive.

At a red light, Eleanor considers whether to make her last stop, to pick up the guest she's asked to speak at the luncheon.

He is a young loan officer at the bank, really no more than a child. She'd learned of his insane dedication to a local aquarium in their last meeting about her payment schedule.

He is waiting, she knows, eager to impress the crowd, to introduce them to the object of his unaccountable affection: a new "charity" for them to consider.

Her hope has been to foster his favor. He would talk to the women of exotic fish, of intractable mollusks, and of school

children's love for them, then beg and receive their money. Checks
in fifty dollar sums would be written: enough to make a mark, but
not enough to miss.

From this invitation, Eleanor has thought she might curry
some grace for her latest loan evasions—a return on her investment.
As she comes to a stop light, as the midday sun beats down on
her, as the hydrangeas mock her from the floorboard, all, at once,
seems far too small.

She lets the engine idle at the thought and has to be honked
at when the signal changes.

But instead of turning left toward the bank to pick up the child
loan officer, she sets her jaw and carries on through the intersection.

The club house is an Italianate fright of wildly pitched angles,
over-shingled eaves, chipped-chalk brick, and yellow casement
storm windows. A mansard roof, as tall as the two floors of the
structure itself, rests like a stovepipe hat upon a frieze depicting
ugly women with jug-like urns on their heads.

Eleanor makes her way to the Palatine Room, its walls decorated
with alternating mirrors and pilasters, its carpeted expanse peopled
with the ageing and the ageless, lunching. A palette of pastels, the
women sit around circular tables on ladder-back chairs atop rose-
colored cushions.

The luncheon is a monthly affair, founded by the late mayor:
an assembly of well-heeled, civic-minded ladies with the historically
bylawed purpose of promoting local business.

But despite the disastrous financial climate, and to Eleanor's
deep dismay, the club's mandate has been changed recently. Instead
of helping entrepreneurs in their time of greatest need, charities
have become the exclusive focus of the group's concerns, showcasing
them in the monthly forums.

In such times, it was posited, philanthropies needed support more than ever. No longer were business people like Eleanor allowed to promote local trades to garner help for their gasping affairs. Now humanitarians of every stripe sob out the difficulties they face since all the money has dried up.

And on what grounds could someone like Eleanor object?

You're going under? Can't pay your creditors? They'd respond: *Well, we have brain disease. Top that.*

Charity madness has energized the club's members, in fact; they've taken on the novel vocabulary of the non-profits and speak it with the gusto of the newly bilingual: "501(c)(3)," they like to say; "fiduciary duty," they enjoy throwing about.

Eleanor steals herself, takes her place at the appointed table, nods to those who greet her.

Her guest will be late, she says.

They're to carry on without him.

If need be, she will speak to the club in his place.

But only if need be.

Luckily, she has not given the boy her phone number, so he can't trouble her with questions as to where she is and whether he should come on his own.

He'll have to figure it out for himself; perhaps by then it will be too late.

She'll have already spoken in his place; she'll have already taken the much-needed opportunity to remind them all of exactly who she is; of exactly what she's borne, of exactly what she stands in want of. A few lies to the boy about the unforeseen circumstances that kept her from calling—a stalled car or a dead phone battery—will smooth things over.

At any rate, it's worth the risk.

The others smile and turn back to their talk. Eleanor surveys the four, already tired of their chatter.

She has known these women her whole life: Margaret, thin and ugly, Anne, thin and pretty; Sissy, simply thin, and Claudia, simply fat. To the person, their families and businesses are now struggling; this she knows from her role as Chamber of Commerce secretary, which gives her access, if not privilege, to the municipality's financial projections.

But these women do not publicly admit their plights, as others are primarily responsible for them. In fact, they constantly ask her to volunteer for things—free of charge, but full of time. To the person, they push these "opportunities" as though they were God's own commandment, talking about the great "needs" in their community and of the wonderful chances to "serve" it.

And not one of them has ordered anything from her shop in months, she thinks—save for Margaret, who'd bought a set of cheap, daisy bud vases for her daughter's birthday party.

Eleanor flushes at the thought.

The salad comes, a mélange of artichokes and grape tomatoes and acidy vinaigrette that she truly despises. Eleanor arms herself with the cutlery and sets in, cutting her eyes around the table as they speak of "contribution targets."

Who talks about *her* need? Who serves *her*?

Hasn't she provided—needs met, services afforded—to all of them? And has she ever, even once, complained?

When the time came, after Max's confinement, she'd discreetly stepped behind the counter and stood across from them, tied on the apron and asked: "How may I help you?"

And had that been easy? But she's kept her mouth shut, hasn't she? She's made no scene. She goes out of her way not to embarrass them about being their maid now, not their peer.

So have they forgotten the arrangement? She has "served," all right—she has served well and served long.

But she has been needy too.

Does need.

Will need.

Is it only the diseased and the illiterate who want for help?

Eleanor slaughters the artichoke hearts before her, scraping the plate with her knife.

She's made herself attractive for them—she's made herself deserving. She isn't scary—not somebody you'd roll the car windows up against. And she doesn't make you feel guilty either, like those African children do.

Besides, it wouldn't have gone on forever. They could have pointed to her as a success—the brave little girl with the crooked spine that they'd bought a brace for, and look at her now! Walking as pretty as you please . . .

The waiter brings the entrée—medallions of beef.

Eleanor breathes hard, blowing like a bull in a loading chute. She has the urge to pick up the meat with her hands and tear a hank of it off with her teeth.

"You know about the opportunity at the Nature Preserve?"

Eleanor's eyes flash. She looks up.

Margaret, thin and ugly.

"About what they're doing with the children there?"

"Yes. It's fantastic," says Anne. "I'll invite the preserve's director when it's my turn to get the speaker."

"Well, you can't," says Margaret. "I've already asked him. He's coming next month."

Anne smiles in a way too wide for the amount of teeth in her mouth. She is about to say something when Claudia asks what opportunity they were speaking of.

"A donor can have a ceremony," explains Margaret. "And he can participate if he likes, along with some school children from across the street, who get to plant it with him as part of an enrichment module."

Eleanor does not wait for a pause in the conversation. Instead, she interrupts to explain that such an arrangement is a clear violation of every child labor law on the books. As a businesswoman, she can speak with authority on the matter.

"What?" Margaret asks.

Eleanor sets down her cutlery, drags the napkin across her mouth with a hard swipe.

"It is."

Sissy frowns. "Oh, now. I'm sure that's not—"

"Absolutely," continues Eleanor. "I'm surprised the protective services agency hasn't been called."

She considers this for a moment, then nods.

"I'm sure it will be. I wouldn't want to be a part of that when it happens."

"I don't think—"

"Oh, absolutely. Absolutely. You better stay well clear."

Margaret holds her stare. Eleanor is emboldened.

"On top of that—who *are* these men anyway? The ones they have planting the trees there? What do you know about them? I wouldn't let my child plant a tree with some strange man in the middle of the woods—"

"They're hardly in the middle of—"

"Not with all the perverts running around. The school's just asking for trouble."

Margaret hesitates, but has the temerity to offer an alternative.

"Well, you could at least donate a tree and say you want the men to put it in themselves without the children, so you—"

"I don't take any pleasure in saying this, but those trees are diseased. I know what I'm talking about. It *is* my business you know."

She cuts her eyes around the circle.

"You all *know* it's my business. The trees they put in are from the cheapest, weakest varietal strains. That way, once you've bought one and had some poor soul's name stuck beside it, you'll have to replace it when it dies. Who would leave a marker beside a *dead* tree? No. Trust me. The trees are meant to die so they can keep you coming back."

After a moment, Claudia asks if Eleanor truly believes such a thing.

"Of course I do. How hard is it to make a hardy tree live, let alone a cheap one?"

Eleanor knows the state of their yards; she knows their feeble attempts and paltry accomplishments—their sad, pale, Home-and-Garden panoramas.

"How many Bradford pears have died in your own yards? How many flowering cherries?" She sneers, shakes her head. "They get you coming and going."

"Well," says Sissy, "I have to agree with Eleanor. Not for the same reasons, of course. But it's more productive to give money straight to a foundation—for research against whatever it was that killed the person."

Eleanor smirks.

"That only encourages the disease," she says. "The researchers get lazy. They should be made to work for their money and produce results; if you feed them all the time, it's in their interest not to cure anything."

Despite their silence, Eleanor presses on, teaches further.

She brings news that cancer is nearly licked, at least the more inconvenient kinds that make you lose your hair and eyebrows and cause you to vomit. She also explains that nobody worries about heart problems anymore, what with the new statins. Diabetes is just a matter of being fat—she cuts a glance at Claudia—and who couldn't stand to lose a little weight?

Claudia says nothing for the rest of the meal.

"I also give to my alma mater," says Sissy. "You can't fault that—"

But she can, and on the same grounds.

"Education is the biggest racket in America. They only feather their nests with the endowments. And you can't tell me that these children know how to read and write and work math. All the teachers do is run them outside to plant trees with sex maniacs. And college is just a booze and prostitution racket underwritten by the vice industries. They come out alcoholic, meth-headed syphilitics, and trained to do nothing but stay in their parents' houses, on their parents' insurance. Just try to tell me I'm wrong. Go ahead."

Since she knows all of their children live at home, and at least one is syphilitic, not a word can be said against her.

When dessert comes, Eleanor is somewhat exhilarated.

She has trounced the frontier. She has beaten back the jungle.

There is one more venture made when coffee is re-poured and a mint dish passed about: a donation to the library. But Eleanor savages the attempt with the fact that handheld readers will soon kill the book industry anyway. Libraries will be pulled down. Besides, for the same educational arguments she's just made, no one can read anyway. Which is all the school's fault. And the Nature Preserve's.

Silence reigns until the phone begins to vibrate in her lap. She would ignore it, but it might be one of her sons.

She has to excuse herself to take it in the hallway.

The call has been a source of dread for a week; it has robbed her of sleep and taken her appetite.

But now, as she walks into the mirrored corridor, her mind floats clear.

For the first time in months, she does not feel as if she will burst through her skin.

It is funny, though, that were it not for the caller ID, she could never tell which son has phoned—at least not until he identified himself in some way. Their voices are the same, the lawyer and the broker: cool; aloof as they consider whether her existence is sustainable or not—scientists observing a patient who lies on the table before them.

In that, they are like Max, at his last: alive only in his voice, but able to do much with that voice—unable, even then, to resist doing whatever he could do.

Naturally, she had been the only one who knew he was faking the extent of his condition.

He hadn't been demented at all, like the doctors loved to say.

He'd been exactly what he always was, in full possession of his faculties, though limited in their use.

For instance, he'd lain there on that bed—able to say only a few things, true—but unable to resist dominating that which was closest.

And that first week, with her sitting there, stunned for once that she was more powerful than he, assuming the unusual place of his wife, he'd said the woman's name.

He'd called it, in fact, instead of Eleanor's.

Though her name had existed silently between them for the length of their marriage—a name assigned to a cheap, faceless rumor—he'd never spoken it out loud in her presence.

And yet, withered, jaundiced, urine-soaked—an insult to

his former self—he'd goaded her with it, as if he'd spent a lifetime waiting for the chance.

But worst of all, he'd said it in a way, in a tone, that Eleanor had never heard coming from herself, let alone him. She had not known him even capable of it.

For he'd said the name with great feeling, with ghostly emotion, with supernatural desire.

In truth, it was more vibration than voice, more note than word. The once dead air had fairly bloomed with the cry; the room was swollen with it, as though the sound of the woman's name was simultaneously both the expression and the fulfillment of his longing.

Eleanor had left the room shaken, then met the blanched faces of a few, now former, friends who had come to offer support and solace—people of known repute, of respectable standing, who had been rudely forced to behold a splendorous miracle, and could not as yet fathom a way out of having to bear witness to it.

"He doesn't know what he's doing," they'd said of him.

"You can't be hurt by what he isn't responsible for meaning," they'd insisted.

"This is the hard part," they'd advised. *"He needs you here."*

"Regardless of whether he deserves it," they had not said, but she had gathered.

So in the end, she'd been trapped in that ministry—bearing the unbearable, otherworldly way in which he'd sustained that name like a chorus, as though it were worthy of such a thing, and the otherworldly way that the chorus sustained him, as though he were.

It has taken great practice to shut out the sound, which echoes still—to contain it, in all its embarrassing enormity.

So as far as "charity" is concerned, as far as "love" is concerned, Eleanor has an opinion.

"Hello," she says into the phone, wondering at her smooth voice, at its newfound vigor.

She waits for her son to answer, whichever one has called. But he does not identify himself, and she has forgotten to look at the display.

Whoever he is, he only tells her to do something:

Quick.

"What?"

Do something. Quick.

"Do *what* quick?"

Anything. Because you're not going to last a month. The spring quarter was more devastating than we knew. Devastating.

Eleanor swallows.

"Do something?"

Quick.

But when she asks again what to do, his answers are all too complicated. Her mind cannot take them in. They involve things that cannot be done quickly—new meetings and new pleas to new bankers and to new investors and to old, old creditors.

Stupefied, Eleanor drifts from the hall, back into the Palatine Room. The lunch has ended and the meeting has begun. The din of voices has dwindled down to one.

Quick? she wonders.

Has he no idea what that word means?

Does he know? Whichever one he is, what can be done quickly and what cannot?

She's directed to the dais and seated, the dead phone still in her hand.

What fools they all are, she thinks.

No one who has experienced what she has would speak as they do.

Life is quick; death is slow. Life starves. Death abounds; it has all the time in the world.

She looks about, at the immortal constancy of the afternoon. She might have been there ten years or twenty, with ten or twenty yet to come.

It is time for the program, it seems.

She is to introduce the speaker in a moment, after the meeting is called to order. After the announcements are made, it seems she is to rise and do something.

"And in memory of the late mayor," says the president, a bland, ignorant woman with broken capillaries in her nose and a husband in receivership, "there's been a suggestion that we take advantage of an opportunity. That is, whether to make an investment at our new Nature Preserve in the name of the late mayor. As he was the greatest benefactor of our mission, it's the least we can do. Plus, since his granddaughter attends the school across the street, it will be a living testament to his memory, to last as long as . . . well, as long as . . ."

Eleanor swallows.

Do something, she thinks.

Her name must have been called; the president must have said something that segued into her standing there, as she found she did, at the podium, in front of her own hydrangea.

The club waits before her, a haze of pastel bulbs in every color, save for one black spot. Because among them now she spies her dark-suited young guest—sitting at her table—in her place. Somehow the banker has arrived on his own initiative. He seems confused but polite, his hands full of brochures on the aquarium, no doubt—ready to speak of his needy fish.

Quick, she tells herself.

Eleanor looks past him, her gaze never catching hold.

Her young friend the banker could not make it this afternoon, she says.

He has been unexpectedly detained.

It is a shame, but these things happen.

Still, she knows what he would do, were he here.

She knows what he would say.

"With regard to what our president has suggested—an 'investment'—at the Nature Preserve, in the 'name' of our late benefactor. My friend would say, he would say . . ."

She looks about at their faces. There they sit, tucked into white linen, sitting behind demitasse, canvassing for charity, creeping ever closer.

"That it won't last."

She smiles.

"All this 'immortal' business we talk about, as though anything this side of creation has ever warranted the language we use: 'For as long as the rivers run' . . . 'For as long as the sun shines' . . . 'Beyond the end of time' . . ."

There. The faces have changed now; they are arrested, shaken.

"Instead, we should give something smaller—an observance, an homage, but nothing more. Because even grief is temporal, and we can't get caught up in spending good money on what are only . . . exotic feelings . . ."

Some have begun to speak to each other—heads meet, ears to mouths.

Eleanor frowns.

"I just mean . . . all I'm saying is . . . we can't act like *girls*, like fourteen-year-old *girls*. We can't mean what we say about 'love' and 'eternity.' Because you know that they won't last."

More are speaking now; they bob together.

"The tree will rot and the pond will be filled in. It's not even . . . practical . . . to invest so much in something . . . in someone . . . you're unsure of. It might not pay off . . . your charity."

They have to hear this. They need to hear it.

"Is it worth that investment?" she asks. "Because you can't be sure. For all you know, behind your back, what you never expected . . . never believed in or dreamed of . . . at least not in the way that . . ."

She stops.

"It can make a fool of you."

A woman in the back—Eleanor cannot tell who—gets up and walks in a light-footed way to the door. She looks as though she is going to get someone, as though she'll return with counterarguments, with people to refute her—priests, bankers, nature preservationists.

"You don't believe that?" Eleanor says, louder now. "That it can make you a fool? Well, it can. It has. It did."

Another gets up to follow the first.

And then she feels the president standing close. She puts her hand on Eleanor's shoulder.

"But that's not the point, or rather, the point is, you can't invest so much in . . . mere *attachments*. Because it might not be justified; it might not be true; it might be a lie."

"Eleanor," the president whispers.

She nods at her name being said—said as it always is, in just the same way, without feeling. Never any different. Never like the way Max had said that woman's name.

"So a nice spray of chrysanthemums," she continues. "That's enough. They last a week or so and then move on. Like you yourself should. Because if it's a mistake, do you really want it memorialized? You want a monument to how big a fool you were to go on adding another branch and another ring every year? You want *that* preserved? In *your* name?"

"Eleanor."

The force on her shoulder is fuller, but the voice, no different. Why should she answer?

"You have to honor them in some passing way . . . a way that doesn't say too much, or mean too much because . . . because *that's* unnatural. It's *unnatural.*"

She nods.

"The dead are provided for. They've got everything they need."

Eleanor stops; the faces before her are dry, pale, wooden, close.

But they look as though they have been expecting someone else—someone more fit, more apt, more deserving of the occasion. As though they see her standing there as always, somewhat above them, but with nothing particularly wanting about her.

Moments pass; she no longer hears the voice at her shoulder.

There is only the pressure of the touch, the weight of not hearing her name called—when all along she has expected to— and the cold, sky blue confusion as to whether it is she that has been deceived or they.

★ ★ ★

AFTER SHE WAS USHERED off the dais, the young banker made his presence known.

He was said to have salvaged the afternoon with his talk on Chinese fighting fish and Caribbean sea anemone.

His talk secured him much support among the diners, and many checks were written to the aquarium in respectable amounts.

But the club's faithlessness toward Eleanor continued long after she had left that day. Their charity could not be rekindled. The decline became an avalanche and then a sluice.

It was said that when she finally went bankrupt, she must have already been ill, despite appearances.

For she had not even attempted to hide her assets or justify her debts, notwithstanding her lawyer's advice. Unaccountably, she had refused to claim either worth or defense and was reduced to the clothes on her back.

In time, her sons placed her in a retirement home near the broker in Charlotte, right after they put her on Medicaid.

Still, she had everything she needed there; she was well attended, well prepared, and well set for the long years to come.

It was also said that when she entered her last sickness, she could still speak, though she often chose not to. In fact, she became particularly taciturn.

The most interest she showed in any conversation was when she was first addressed:

Eleanor.

But her attentions always fell away after that, as though somehow disappointed by voices that could never quite exceed the limits of a natural range.

For Your Listening Pleasure

H E OPENS THE SCREEN DOOR and widens it with the back side of his elbow, his hand held up to keep the blood from . . . What? he wonders—to keep it from what? Dripping? Running too fast? Staining the floor?

It does all of those things anyway, but something tells him that he should hold it up. A trail of bright red spackles follows him across the linoleum.

Chairs are in the way; his sons have left them there. He must kick one aside and then turn his hips to press past the other in order to get to the kitchen sink. The basin is stacked with dirty dishes, and three plates full of half-eaten eggs and toast stare back at him. His gorge rises as he bleeds onto the scraps.

Hot or cold? Which is best for an open cut?

He switches on both and works the fingers back and forth. Or should he do that?

The water blasts against the wound; it feels flat and numb beneath the force, as though he were pressing the heel of his hand against a sheet of glass. The gouge is in the meat of his lower left palm, above his knuckles but below his wrist. It is the lack of pain that frightens him.

Through the window above the sink he sees his neighbor mowing his backyard. It is a March day, too cold, too early and grassless for such noise. And for an instant, it worries him, that the sound is difficult to hear over, should he need to . .

What? Need to what? Call out? But he won't need to call out.

It's not that bad. He won't need to call out.

Still, he is alone in the house, and it is too loud.

He holds his hand in the chalice of the other and pulls it from beneath the stream. The bright red well gushes up through the gored flesh, so he grabs a mostly clean dishrag from the counter. The rough starched cotton resists at first, refuses to absorb the blood, so he wraps it around the hand twice and then steps over to the washing machine and yanks out a soured, sharp-smelling bath towel to hold against it too. He swathes the wound, makes a turban for it, then sits on a chair against the wall and holds the hand between his legs, crushing it hard between his knees.

He will wait a few minutes, to see if it stops; then, if it won't, he'll have to call someone.

But it will stop. Besides, he doesn't want to scare the boys, he doesn't want to be inexplicably gone when they return. But then, he doesn't want to be bleeding all over the house, either.

He looks about the kitchen, notices the splashes of blood on the floor, and several red smears and footprints. He'll have to clean them up before they arrive.

They had not stayed long—only the night before—when their mother had come for them again. Their every-other-weekend visits began Friday after school and lasted until Sunday, after church. But she had wanted them to go to a birthday party at her sister's, and he had relented. Alone most of the day, he had decided to run some errands across town, to get some new sheet music and to pick up his suits from the cleaners. But the trip had taken longer than he expected. He was late returning home, and there had been only an hour to spare before they were due.

He had meant to have hamburgers ready when they got there. At five and three, it was the only thing they would eat, and the only thing he could cook. He had forgotten to buy pizza or chicken fingers at the store, but he always had a steady supply of hamburger. For that reason, he ate them himself a great deal—not because he wanted to, but because they were easy and he was good at cooking them. He made individual patties of the meat, then covered each with plastic wrap and froze them in bulk, like a roll of coins.

He wiggles his fingers.

Why is it still bleeding? Is it because of all the aspirin he takes?

His blood pressure is far too high for a fifty-year-old man; the doctor had said so. He is also too heavy and carries the extra weight around his stomach, which he was informed meant bad things, according to the latest research. The news had come as a shock, and he was taking baby aspirin to supplement his blood thinners. It has also made him more cautious about the boys' health: what they should eat and how it should be prepared. Had he not heard that very week, on television, that it was wrong to microwave things in plastic—that defrosting them that way set off some kind of reaction that caused cancer in lab mice—he would not have stabbed himself. But he had remembered the counsel, one given by a morning show anchor in dire terms and supported by an alarmed physician. So he had taken a butcher knife with him out to the gas grill, in order to separate the patties from each other and defrost them there; it would be faster, it seemed.

To prize them apart, he should have placed the meat on the shelf next to the grate—pressed his hand down on top and worked the blade in between the crevices. But he had thought they would give way easily, so he had just held them in his left. Then he found he had to use more pressure than he ought. When it worked loose, it gave way all at once, opening the way to his left palm.

The blade went deep. And though he snatched it back at once, he saw something horribly white inside before the blood came.

It amazed him how far it sank, how little it hurt, how much fluid it let. The flesh had blown back in tatters, like rubber around a punctured tire.

He opens his knees an inch, to peek at the size of the stain that seeps through the cloth. It is the shape of a chrysanthemum now, but he cannot tell if it has grown any larger. A throbbing has set up in his forearm; that, and a sensation as though the tips of his fingers are held against hot ice.

Maybe that's good; maybe that signifies a brake in the bleeding. A while longer, then; he will wait a while longer.

★ ★ ★

ALREADY HE KNOWS what this means. Even if it is nothing serious, he will be unlikely to use his hand for a time. He hopes he might at least work his fingertips; otherwise, he cannot tune the pianos.

That is mostly what he does now—that, and man the front desk at a restoration company. He can deal with the phones and the computer, even if he has done something bad to his left hand, his weak side. But he needs two in order to manage the tuning. He will be unable to place the rubber mutes in between the strings, or to calibrate the pitch with the hammer. Most of all, he will be unable to manipulate the keys with his left, to sound them as his right adjusts the tension on the pins—one hand calling, the other hand answering, the response moving with, in tandem to, the need. But more than either of those things, without two hands, he cannot play the piano at Ashington's.

There is only him left now, out of a whole staff of players the store had once commissioned to perform. And though he is still at the flagship building downtown, and no one has mentioned anything ominous, this could be a reason to end his engagement. A friend who played at the only other location in the city has been laid off, as the chain is being sold to a larger group that started in the malls. With the change—and in truth, well before then—the work had slowed, become part-time, and then only on Sunday afternoons. There had been a time when it was more.

For thirty years, he played five afternoons a week. With a music degree and some time at a conservatory, his livelihood had consisted of teaching children in the mornings, driving from one suburban school to the next for their music appreciation hour. But just before noon, he had taken the bus downtown to the old department store: gray and neoclassical and huge. With his valise in hand, he had ascended to the mezzanine level by way of the escalator—its interior sides brassed and glossy enough to show the shine of his shoes—to a raised station just to the right, where the piano sat, its lid propped open. Nearby, on top of a faux marble half-pillar, a vase was filled with a huge spray of flowers, changing with the seasons: asters for fall, poinsettias for Christmas, lilies for spring, roses for summer. He would take the dimpled leather bench, draw himself up to the high-glossed piano, its black-and-ivory teeth solid, smooth, tight to the touch. Then he would remove his sheet music from the valise and begin.

In time, he had not really needed the transcriptions. But it was part of the atmosphere, and there was a certain look to the ebony music board propping the crème-colored paper, with its trebles and clefs and shape notes dancing along a harp of lines.

While he played, his eyes would stray from the keys to watch the velvet heads strike at the strings from underneath, like minnows darting up to the surface of a golden pond.

★ ★ ★

THE MUSCLES IN HIS HIPS HURT from the squeezing, so he has to relieve them, release the pressure applied to his hand. He moves the makeshift cast onto the chair, underneath his left thigh, and lets the gravity of his leg hanging down do the work for a while.

If it would just stop long enough for him to bind it up.

He does not look, but the cloth feels wet and greasy against the wound.

A little while longer, he could wait; a while longer yet.

★ ★ ★

THOUGH IT IS MEANT to be something special, the setting is not as grand as it was years ago, when he first began.

Back then, he had been stationed in the penthouse, at the restaurant that overlooked the skyline. No child under eight was admitted, no man without a coat, and no bags could be brought to the tables. And yet, people had flocked there, because the food was excellent but inexpensive—simple salads and sandwiches and soups—and presented on nice plates with linen napkins by mustachioed men in short-waisted coats. For the price of good behavior, they could afford to be treated sumptuously. And off to one side, while the patrons ate and smiled out at the city below, he played for them—his shoulders straight, his foot working the damper—the more romantic tunes of Richard Rodgers, of Cole Porter, of Henry Mancini. Grand, sweeping songs, performed with authority, but not too loud—just enough to provide a float, just enough to afford a cloud upon which to glide—"Moon River," "Lara's Theme," "Fascination."

That was part of the store's appeal, back then, the atmosphere it had wanted to project: cool sophistication, high above the city; an ethereal experience, set to a soaring score. And it was not only to encourage a certain image that they featured music. It was felt and the players were all told that the piano made the most mundane of things—buying boxer shorts, socks, toasters and hand cream—into an ennobling event.

"*Ashington's: Where the Customer is Royalty,*" the sign used to say.

★ ★ ★

H E WITHDRAWS HIS HAND from beneath his leg.
The blossom is fuller now, showy and round. And there is something like a pebble inside his palm: a small rock-like thing, or maybe—his gaze searches the wall as he notes it—a nub of some sort. Worse still, his last two fingers, though he can move them, are distant-feeling, as if they alone lay inside a cool suede glove.

Of course, that could be due to the pressure he has applied.

He places the bundle between his knees again and clamps them shut once more, but with less force.

His head lowers to his chest.

This is what comes of living alone.

★ ★ ★

H E HAD MARRIED AGAIN at a point in his life when he should have known better. The only good thing born of their broken six years union was the children.

It has been a great joy, to have them now, so late. But all the pleasure he takes in them he shares with his dead wife rather than

with the boys' mother. Any pride or amusement they give him—
"Watch his hands" . . . "Look at the way he holds his head"—is
privately shown to a woman who had never seen them, had no
part in their making or raising, was gone years before their birth.
She had been fond of children though, and before she got sick,
traveled about the schools, teaching them how to draw. Every
work was dedicated, she made certain; whatever was accomplished
was meant to please a mother or father, a grandparent or a friend,
and part of each project was in discerning how to go about that
task—what would the object of the work's dedication want most?

He had been made to wait until she finished her lesson—music
following art. And as he stood in the door or sat at a small desk, he
had watched her glide about the room, her slight figure bending
over a child's shoulder, her thick blonde hair thrown back from
her face and caught at one side by her hand. This had caught his
attention, the earnestness with which she sought to instill, not
only color and design, but the duty to delight.

So whenever he sees his sons do something that would have
pleased her, it is she he would collude with. And since he has
never considered the boys' mother anyone whom he truly knew,
or who truly knew him, there is no betrayal in this. She was never
any real part of his life, his ex-wife, a young girl from Eastern
Europe, strangely naïve about the prospects of an American man
in his mid-forties.

She had made her livelihood giving thirty-minute lessons on
a rented upright, and she needed it tuned from time to time. He
should have known, from all he had seen, that the claustrophobia
of such work, the sheer thanklessness of it, could drive someone
to desperation. But having lived by himself for so long, he was
prey to her ambitions—for herself, for him: that he could start

his own music store; that he could play for a symphony; that he was not too old and unknown for concert dates to be a possibility.

Deep down, he had not taken these things seriously, though he had been flattered by them. And had he not been converted by his lust, he would never have taken her to bed; certainly never married.

But she had gotten pregnant, and the enormity of such a thing had made him over completely. To enlarge his income, he had secured the job at the restoration company, supplemented it with the tuning, and devoted himself to the marvel of such a future. Another son, soon after the first, had only redoubled his determination; but hers redoubled too. Rather than end her ambitions, the children had only increased them. Her ideas became a fixation: he must talk to the bank about a business loan; he must audition for a major conductor; he must compose his own music instead of playing that of others.

He resisted these things, fantastic as they were, and this bred her contempt. His lack of determination was unbelievable, she said. He was un-American; she was more American than he.

★ ★ ★

THE TOWEL IS MUSKY and greasy now, and the stain, an old, rust red.

He cannot be a fool about it; he cannot let himself bleed any more. And even if it has slowed or stopped inside the mashed cocoon of cloth, something is not right. The last two fingers are aliens to the rest. They float clear of his hand, phantoms that haunt their native place.

He gets up and begins to walk to the counter. His head feels light, his feet too far from his body. But this could be his imagination, or the effect of rising too swiftly.

His aim is imperfect as well when he reaches for the drawer where he keeps the boys' colors and scissors and glue.

He rummages around inside the pile of supplies and finds a ring of masking tape. Then he steps over to the sink, starts the faucet, and pulls the bundling from his hand.

The blood wells up again, but not as forcefully as before; it seeps above the fractured flesh like water sweating through cracked hide. He rewashes the wound, dries it the best he can with paper towels. Then he hooks the end of the tape to the inside base of his thumb, loops it over the back of his hand, and begins to seal the gouge to itself by wrapping it over and over.

But the flesh is still damp, the wound not dry enough to tack the tape. It slips back and forth as he works. In the end, it is useless, a rope of slick cord that will not bind anything; what's more, the handling unloosens some vessel that had clotted, so that now the flow is stronger, dribbling down his frozen wrist.

The mower is silent outside; when he looks, no one is in his neighbor's yard. He had not noticed how quiet things had grown.

He finds another towel, holds it against his hand.

He must call; he must let someone know.

★ ★ ★

TIMES CHANGE; he is aware of that. It so happens that he does not like the present as much as he had the past, but others seem to. If the atmosphere is less important than the product now, if the fluidity of the traffic flow trumps the tenor of the ambiance, that is the decision of those who know more than he, and whose investment is at risk all the while. He concedes that; he is not angry.

When they closed the restaurant in the penthouse, he had not complained; when they moved the piano from station to station, down and down, further and further from the top floor, he had not said a word. And now, if it all ends, it is not for him to object. Besides, it is not that he regrets the loss of the piano so much. What he will miss is what it has allowed him to do: to serve in the background.

That is all he wanted, really. That is the most he has asked for. Next to him, a placard on an easel: "For your listening pleasure . . ."— just those few words and nothing more, certainly not his name.

Because he was not a feature, but a support—part of the whole, not at the center circle, in the wings, not on the stage—people gave him the shadows of their attention. They were soothed and glorified in an unconscious way by his labor, as though pleased in their sleep by a light wind passing through a screen door. While the others worked and toiled to sell their wares, sunken in the hard transaction of words, he provided a softening milieu, a medial charm. There was a sacral purity to it. People floated up and down the escalator past his offerings, his songs in a major key. And their eyes, for however long, blessed him with a benediction. He gave them that; a chance to do that.

★ ★ ★

His neighbor has left; his car is gone. Somehow, he had not heard the car start, despite how loud his muffler is. And he does not know the people on the other side of him or those across the street.

He does not think he can drive himself; or rather, he does not think he should. He does not trust his left hand to work right, and his transmission is manual. Besides, although he is unsteady, mostly from fear of what to do—how to handle the boys—he cannot risk fainting as he drives.

He must hold the receiver in his right hand and use his thumb to mash in the buttons. He makes a mistake, must hang up, start over.

He calls her cell phone first. But she does not answer, and her mailbox is full. Appointments, most likely; mothers making and changing and canceling their children's piano lessons. So he calls to leave a message on her machine at home, to say where he will be and why.

"At the emergency room . . . about to call them now . . . nothing to be afraid of . . ."

But what if she does not get the message? What if she brings the boys here, straight from the party?

He has had to throw two sheets away, though he was nearly done with the note, because he has smudged them with blood. He does not want them to be afraid of that—of blood-smeared paper. So he has to clean and dry his right hand as well, and hold the paper still with his left elbow, to keep his hand clear of the note as he scribbles where he will have gone.

Should he put it on the door? Or should he leave it on the table inside?

"I'm sorry," he begins, "I had to . . ."

What? Leave?

"I hurt myself and had to go to the . . ."

Where? Where would they take him?

"I'll make this up to you," he writes.

★ ★ ★

SAMI, A SMILING BALD MAN from New Delhi, runs the jewelry department across from the piano. He wears dark shirts beneath dark suits to set in relief his florid silk ties. He is a ballroom dancer who waltzes his wife around polished gymnasium floors on the weekends. But the weekdays he spends with his mistress, Dorinda, a tiny wrinkled woman with ink-black hair, teased high and caught at the neck with a gigantic bow. She sells furs, sables and ermines, to old ladies and rich Arabs, and tips Sami off whenever they are in the store. When he is not holding a woman's hand to slip a cocktail ring onto it, cooing at the velvet texture of her skin, he will lean across the counter and call out.

"Oh, my friend, my friend," he will say, after "Love Is a Many Splendored Thing"—majestic, windblown, cliff-perched. "Play *that* one again. There's a rich lady over in furs right now—she'll *have* to have a ring if you break her heart with *that* one."

He would only smile and shake his head, because he refuses to repeat himself. He has a rotation. But he will do what he can to help Sami without ruining his order.

"Here she comes," Sami would say, as the woman emerged from the furriers. "Come, my friend. Make her stop. Play something loud and gorgeous to make her stop."

And as Sami stands at attention, beaming his smile upon the approaching woman, he might segue into "A Time for Us" or "The Summer of '42."

"Ohhhhh, Madam," Sami would swoon, "How lovely! Allow me to at least *see* you in these diamonds while your song is all about us. That is all—just let me *see* you!"

In the old days, when closing time rolled around and he had put his sheet music away, the store manager took the time to walk by and thank them for the day's work, for the role they had played in it. He would stop—a small, fastidious man in red bow ties who held his hands behind his back—and ask what had sold well that day, or what had been the mood of the clientele.

In time, the clerks and staff would congregate. With the lights dimming, the buffers and floor waxers at work, the great place was retired for the evening in peaceful stages. Especially at Christmas, especially during the big summer and winter sales, they would slowly gather from their respective stations—descending staircases, rising up lifts—to mill about the piano in a satisfied fatigue.

"She went to you after me, didn't she? I saw her."

"You couldn't talk him out of it. He wanted that shirt with that suit."

"Tomorrow will be busier than today, if that's possible."

"Yes."

"Tomorrow."

"We'll do it all again."

★ ★ ★

I HURT MYSELF," HE says to the operator.

. . . "What? I cut myself. My hand. With a . . ."

. . . "No. I didn't mean to."

. . . "I need someone to come. I feel like . . . I shouldn't drive."

. . . "There's no one here. It's only me. And nobody . . ."

. . . "Just send someone. Please."

The bleeding has stanched somewhat; the towels he holds against it remain mostly dry. But less and less does he own his fingers, and now he feels a strange, weakening line in his hand, as though it were being slowly drawn thin, like gum stretched from a rope into a wisp. The whole arm is heavy, and the muscles in his shoulder ache.

He mops up the kitchen as best he can, locks the back door and goes outside to tape the note to the front. It will not stick to the dusty wood, though, and he has to close the paper between the screen door and the frame. But then he realizes he is trapped outside, there on the porch, because he cannot go back in, lest the note fall off.

So he sits on the front steps, his bundled arm hanging down like a package he must relay, and waits.

★ ★ ★

WHY DID IT PLEASE HIM? To be this? To be "only this," as his ex-wife would have put it. He could never have explained it to her. To further a greater glory, to people the attendant world—ministering in his service. That is what he finds most pleasing: the placement of the spoon; the turning of the bed clothes; the pouring of the high tea. He had aspired to be a waiter, at one point, long ago; at a large ancient restaurant, carrying in flaming desserts and uncorking old champagne. He had aspired to be a footman for the queen, a doorman at a grand hotel, always making the majesty more majestic. Polishing the silver or driving the carriage—that was what he wanted, and at Ashington's, had received.

But his last wife had not understood what his first wife had never needed to be told. Even at her sickest, she had not tired of his narrations of the day, of the feel he had taken of the atmosphere they created. She was not interested in the praise he had received, or how he might transform it into some kind of prosperity.

When she had grown too weak to wash her own hair, she would smile and ask him to do it, listing in detail how he might perform the service. He noted with care all the preparations, all that she would have him do.

First, he would place the chair back against the lavatory and ease her into the seat. Then, cushioning her spine with one hand and her skull with the other, he would lay her neck against the towel-lined bowl. He would have already tested the temperature, on the skin against his wrist; he would have already gauged the water's flow. And as he wet and lathered the patches of thin, fragile hair with his fingertips, he watched her face relax into a phrase of distant pleasure; an air of reflexive content. He spoke in dulcet tones as she rested there, his voice as measured and rhythmic as his touch.

She would nod from time to time, at his recital of what they had brought off in the store that day, of what they had accomplished—each movement, each progress. And whenever she stirred, roused herself to ask him a question, it was never of what he had done himself, but of what the store was doing, or what the people had most enjoyed.

At times, she would suggest things she had heard on the radio, while she lay in bed—songs they might like, things for him to practice. She made ways of remembering the titles and tunes so she could relate them later without having to write them down.

In the evenings, after he had played one of her suggestions, he would slip into her room and hum the theme.

"It Might as Well Be Spring."

Her eyes would open in sympathetic vibration—string calling string.

"How had they liked it?" she had asked. "Which had pleased them most?"

In the end, she never asked him what he would do about this or that, but what *they* should, though it was clear he would have to make such decisions by himself, very soon. Even toward the last, she had not worried him with the solitariness to come. She had not confronted him with that; she had been good and graceful in ignoring it, in not speaking of it.

And she had not thanked him for washing her hair.

★ ★ ★

His neighbor's dogs are in his back yard. He can hear them back there, two small hounds attracted to the meat he has left at the grill. Short, they are clamoring to reach high enough, jumping up—their paws scratching the metal—and falling back again.

They will have it, in time; they will not stop until their teeth reach a corner of the plastic, snatch the roll off the grill and onto the ground. And then they will fight.

But he has no mind for them now, no heart to rise and walk back there, nor even to shout; he is removed from that. It seems a long time ago, though it cannot have been more than half an hour.

Things are reduced, funneled, so that he hears his own steady breathing, and is conscious of how seldom cars have passed.

★ ★ ★

The engagement would end now, before he had meant for it to. They would have the whole thing packed up when he came back, if he ever did. There would be a portable kiosk there, where the piano had stood, some modular station devoted to seasonal items—potpourri or gardening accessories, since it was spring—something to catch the eye as the customers rode past. Even Sami had said it was coming. He had seen the kiosks popping up around the store, displacing counters that had been there for years.

He could still play at weddings; he could still play for birthday parties. He could, if they would let him. But there were not so many events or places that needed that anymore. And the ones already in the field were jealous of their territory.

Besides, people often wanted more than just a pianist, they wanted a combo—jazz, which he did not play, or if not jazz,

a string quartet. He did not really play classical music either—
something his ex-wife would never accept.

No. He played themes.

He played scores.

He played the kind of music that Ashington's Department
Store entertained its customers with, of a Sunday afternoon, as
they rode the escalator, up and down.

★ ★ ★

IT IS COOL OUTSIDE, the March sun too weak to melt the chill
from the air, to drive the high clouds from the sky. But the
light is strong when it breaks through the cover. It falls in gallant
waves, rallying in pulses of gold before the clouds take it again. As
he waits, he watches the changes, the swell and fall, the advance
and retreat.

And at length he remembers what he had felt when he
withdrew the knife, when he glimpsed the strange white thing
inside his hand: a twinge, like a split chord or a quivering line.
The snap had set up an odd glow in his arm, a nimbus or a halo,
a corona that had centered his attention, became all feeling, but at
the same time became all feeling's loss: at once the focus, so that he
felt nothing else, but also the end, as if to signal its leaving—one
octave high, to call, one octave low, to depart.

The glut of blood that rushed into the space had broken
his notice, detached it and brought him back to the immediate
crisis—the sight of the red suffusion, of the liquid surfeit, having
more power over his attention than the loss of his touch.

But now he remembers. And now he leans into the memory,
his gaze fastened to what he must see.

There is a point in the departure at which all is present, all
has never been more effulgent or replete. And it comes in a strange

inversion, in what might be the opposite of itself—in a bestowal that seems like receipt—as one who has sought to please must suffer the gifts of others.

It is spied in the tolerance of pointless news, the patience at awkward visits, the endless good faith left at the bedside, like parched and wilting bouquets. It is in the charity of tired, forbearing eyes, enduring the customs of courtesy, of letting others do what they will, what they must.

His gaze follows the sun as it shimmers across the grass in its leaving.

He had planned to teach the boys how to play, so that they would know how to please, how they could experience the pleasure in giving such a thing.

But now he knows he must teach them something else, now he must show them this, what he has so late learned from his master class: the steel with which one must hold himself as he is played upon—not well, not classically—but intently as the medium of devotion, as the instrument and object of joy.

★ ★ ★

THERE IS NO SIREN when they pull down the street. They drive surprisingly slow. But there is no real emergency, he has told them; he is only erring on the side of caution.

They park at the curb in front of him, then get out of the ambulance at an unhurried pace. Two men in white shirts and white pants; one is in sunglasses, the other wears headphones.

Still, they look kind; they smile. His throat is tight, or he would greet them.

The back doors of the van come open. The men take out their kits.

And as they approach, he takes a breath. He relaxes his

shoulders, then his chest. He must play the left now, they the right. He will sound, and they will respond, and in the end, maybe there is little difference in the two.

Still, he must have something to say, when they ask him what they will. He must prepare himself to bestow this passive grace. He is obliged to, so that they can have their chance, to perform as they must.

He places his hurt hand in the brace of his right, begins to lift it, for their use.

And as they come to stand before him—two white figures with two black kits—his thoughts turn to possibilities: so that he will have a need, when they search for how they can help. He will have a want, when they ask what they can do for him. He will have a request, when they wonder what he would like to hear.

A.G. Harmon's fiction, essays, and reviews have appeared in *Triquarterly, the Antioch Review, Shenandoah, the Bellingham Review, St. Katherine Review, Image,* and *Commonweal,* among others. His fiction won the 2001 Peter Taylor Prize (*A House All Stilled,* University of Tennessee Press, 2002) and was the runner-up for the 2007 William Faulkner Prize for the Novel. His academic work,  *Eternal Bonds, True Contracts: Law and Nature in Shakespeare's Problem Plays* was published by SUNY Press. He was a 2003 Walter Dakin fellow at the Sewanee Writers' Conference. He grew up on horse-and-cattle farms in Mississippi and Tennessee. Currently, he teaches at The Catholic University of America in Washington, DC.

ALSO FROM WORD GALAXY PRESS

Margaret Rockwell Finch, *Crone's Wines: Late Poems*

Emily Grosholz, *The Stars of Earth: New and Selected Poems*

Elizabyth A. Hiscox, *Reassurance in Negative Space – Poems*

www.wordgalaxy.com

www.ingramcontent.com/pod-product-compliance
Lightning Source LLC
Chambersburg PA
CBHW022207030726
47494CB00021B/2066